The Candy Shoppe

Dorothy Abel

HARVEST HOUSE PUBLISHERS
Eugene, Oregon 97402

THE CANDY SHOPPE

Copyright © 1983 by Harvest House Publishers
Eugene, Oregon 97402

Library of Congress Catalog Card Number 83-080876
ISBN 0-89081-388-4

Printed in the United States of America.

To my husband, Al

LOVE

A small boy went into a pet shop. "Mister," he addressed the manager, "I want to buy that puppy."

The proprietor followed the pointed finger to the little crippled dog all by himself. "Son," he replied, "that puppy is worthless. We're going to have him put to sleep in the next few days."

"But," the would-be owner answered, "I have saved my money just to buy that one puppy. I have been looking at him in the window every day. He's the only one I want."

Once again the manager of the store explained the problem—the dog was crippled and worthless, and would be put to sleep. The small chap then reached down with two little hands and pulled up his trousers. The man observed two little legs enclosed in braces. "Mister," he said, "you don't know what love can do!"

—Cecil Clegg

Taken from *Proclaim*, Copyright © 1981 by The Sunday School Board of the Southern Baptist Convention, page 33. Used by permission.

Chapter 1

Even the long, jagged crack near the end of the black marble soda fountain couldn't mar the charm and beauty of the quaint old shop I worked in. A cool, refreshing glimpse of the early 1900s greeted your eye when you stepped inside from the noisy, bustling street. From the intricately fashioned carvings of the mahogany woodwork high above the sparkling glass candy cases to the long mirrored wall behind the gleaming ice cream bar, you could easily forget the pressures of the fast-paced world and sit down to chat with friends in a most relaxed atmosphere. You could sit in old-fashioned ice cream parlor chairs at small circular tables and attack a triple banana split with your choice of ice cream flavors and toppings. While enjoying your treat, you could quietly put aside such recent problems as the high cost of gasoline and the apparent dishonesty in government.

Whether it was the casual, sweet-smelling atmosphere or the kindly, homespun philosophies of the elderly gentleman who owned it, people often flocked to Reed's Candy Shoppe—young people, old people, happy people, busy people. Nearby employees, local shoppers, established customers—almost everyone, it seemed, had time and money enough for such delights as a box of assorted bonbons and creams or a chocolate marshmallow sundae, plus a few words of gentle wisdom from the proprietor.

The door of the old shop jingled open and a gush of warm spring air poured over the fountain. I looked up. It was wealthy Mrs. Haysley. I glanced across the store at Bertha. She was still restocking trays of orange and lemon slices behind a candy case. She appeared not to notice the elderly, well-groomed arrival.

Mrs. Haysley marched over the darkly tiled floor and placed her trim figure on one of the red leather stools that lined the long soda fountain. I greeted her with a smile and a glass of chilled water.

"Afternoon, dear." She sipped the water and cast a quick look around.

I pretended not to notice her searching expression, but I knew very well that she was looking for Mr. Reed. Bertha had told me that she had been in the shop almost every day since Mr. Reed's wife had died some months earlier. She was later than usual today. I smiled to myself. Mrs. Haysley had learned quickly that the best time to catch Mr. Reed in the store was during the morning. Afternoons he was in the back of the shop making his delicious ice cream and candy, or he was off somewhere running errands and delivering candy orders.

"What will you have?"

"I'll have a fruit salad sundae, dear."

While I filled her request, she slid down from the tall stool, patted her neat, silver curls, and paraded about in her expensive tailored dress. She peered into the candy cases along the opposite wall and glanced repeatedly beyond the small tables and chairs at the mirrored wall across the back of the store. Narrow doors that flanked each side of the mirror led to the storage-and-preparation area and to Mr. Reed's office and a comfortable lounge. Once Mrs. Haysley stopped to pass the time with my co-worker, who, I observed, had finished her refilling chore and stood in the back corner by the telephone wearing a look of smug satisfaction on her plump face.

When Mrs. Haysley returned to the fountain, she sat nibbling at the sundae I had made while the jangle of the front door brought me another customer. Later, when I came back to the elderly woman, she laid down her spoon and reached into her purse, emerging with an alligator wallet.

"Where's Mr. Reed today, Holly?" she asked while extracting a 20-dollar bill.

"He went out a few minutes ago," I said from the cash register.

She tried to hide her disappointment behind a poised expression, but I saw it darkening her bespectacled eyes.

"He probably won't be gone long," I added, "unless he got to talking to someone. He just went around the corner to the bank."

A ray of light welled up behind Mrs. Haysley's wire-framed glasses. "He went to the bank? Oh, my, what a coincidence. I was on the way down there myself."

She finished her sundae in two extremely large and unbecom-

ing gulps, then jumped down and hastened toward the door.
"I'll see you girls later," she bubbled.

"Wait!" I called, leaning over the fountain, "you forgot your
change!"

She retraced her steps. "Oh, yes. How silly of me."

As soon as Mrs. Haysley had gone, Bertha came trotting over
to me. Bertha was unusually tall, and she overflowed with suntan flesh, which she acquired from weekends spent outdoors.

"That Abigail Haysley makes me sick!" she announced. "She
thinks she's so cool, but she doesn't have me fooled for a
minute. I know she's set her bonnet for ol' Mr. Reed."

"Is that such a terrible thing?" I asked as I wiped the marble counter clean and deposited Mrs. Haysley's dish in a sink
of sudsy water.

"She's buried two husbands already," Bertha informed me,
her indignation clearly visible, "and now she's living high on
what they left her. She probably drives them to an early grave
just so she can go off in hot pursuit of someone else."

I laughed at Bertha's ridiculous chidings. "You make her
sound just awful. She seems like a nice old lady to me."

Bertha folded her arms and hunched her shoulders, making
her long neck seem short, and in spite of her youthfulness (she
was a mere 19 while I was a matronly 22), she stood glaring
at me for all the world like a wise and ancient turtle. "You mark
my words, Holly—she'll find a way to hook ol' Mr. Reed and
she'll do it before he even knows what's happened."

Before I could comment, the front door chimed open and
in came Linda Benton from the loan department of the large
bank around the corner. It was a hobby of mine to study the
origins of names and discover their meanings. Linda was a
Spanish name and it meant "beautiful." Linda Benton certainly
lived up to her name. With shoulder-length blonde hair, deep

velvet-brown eyes, and bright-smiling lips, she could look at you for all the world like a playful kitten wrapped in a ball of soft yarn.

Linda bounced up to the fountain and climbed on a stool in front of us. "Fix me a vanilla shake, will you, Holly? And hurry up—I don't have much time. I'm on a short break."

"Sure," I said, and moved away as she began to whirl around on the stool. "Bertha, have I got something to tell you!" said Linda, suddenly spinning to a halt. "Guess who I'm going out with tonight?"

Bertha squealed and I nearly dropped the shake can. "Oh, Linda, are you really?"

"He asked me this morning at the coffee machine."

"You're so lucky. I'd give anything if he'd ask me out!" Bertha sighed romantically. "I wonder where he'll take you?"

"Who cares as long as I'm with *him*?" crooned Linda, her deep velvet eyes aglow with delight.

"As long as you're with *him*?" I asked, setting her milkshake on the counter.

She pulled the straw around to her shiny lips and took a long drink before giving me an answer. "Michael Britton, of course."

"He's the banker's son, isn't he?"

Linda laid 70 cents on the counter. "One of them."

I looked from Linda to Bertha. "You two talk about this guy so much, but I never see him." I focused a sharp eye on my fellow employee. "I thought you said he comes in here a lot."

"He does, but you just started working here last week. Give him a chance."

"He came down here yesterday," Linda said, " 'cause he asked me to come with him, but I had some past-due notices to get out."

"Oh, yeah, he did," Bertha said with marked coolness. "He was in here while you were in the lounge eating lunch, Holly."

"Why didn't you come and get me?"

"No way. I want to keep you hidden from him as long as possible."

Linda giggled frivolously. "You're prettier than she is, and Bertha can't stand the competition."

"One look at you and your big green eyes and long black hair and I've had it forever," said Bertha.

I appreciated the compliments of my new acquaintances, but I had never considered myself that attractive. I had always thought my nose was a little too big for my face, but I was glad that other people didn't seem to be overly conscious of it. And I didn't like the color of my eyes. They were green, as Bertha mentioned, but not that pretty emerald green. They were more of a dark, murky shade, always reminding me of the scum found floating on farm ponds. I suppose with my dark hair and rather gloomy eyes I could look quite sad and mysterious, but I seldom did. I had been taught that life was an attitude, and than an open, cheery disposition reaped the greatest benefit.

"Beside you, I don't stand a chance," Bertha added.

I looked from Bertha to Linda and then back at Bertha. I doubted if she ever stood much of a chance with the young man in question, but for once I didn't blurt out what was on my mind.

"I'm bound to see this guy sooner or later, and I admit I'm a little curious," I said. "The way you two talk he must be the most noticeable man alive."

"After Robert Redford," Bertha said.

"Robert Redford's nice-looking," I said offhand. "He has a pretty smile."

"Michael's not the Robert Redford type," Bertha went on.

"For one thing, he's got dark hair. Now Leroy—"

"Who's Leroy?"

"Michael's brother, but...you wouldn't be interested in him."

"Because he looks like Robert Redford?"

"It's not that, " Linda said. "Nobody's much interested in him—in dating him, I mean."

"Why not?"

"He's crippled," Bertha replied. "He had polio when he was a kid."

"Oh, that's too bad."

"I think it's the pits," Linda said, " 'cause Leroy's a super nice guy and is he ever good-looking. He's my boss at the bank, a vice-president, and you couldn't ask for a better person to work for."

"Yeah, but his legs are paralyzed," Bertha added. "Who'd want a man like that?"

"He gets around all right on crutches," Linda said, "but I'd rather go out with his brother."

The front door jingled open and two lively youngsters scampered up to the fountain. I moved to wait on them and dismissed the Britton brother from my mind.

It was almost closing time when Mr. Reed returned with an engrossing tale about how he had accidentally run into Mrs. Haysley at the bank and how she had asked him to go with her to the local hardware store where she purchased a heating element for her hot water heater.

"I'll stop by her house on my way home," the old gentleman told us. "She's a widow, you know, and she said she doesn't know anybody who'll come this late to fix her water heater."

I watched Bertha roll her dark, expressive eyes in exasperation. I smiled, amused at her obvious concern.

"Why didn't she think about that this morning?" my co-worker asked. "She would've had plenty of time to get someone to fix it."

"I don't know," Mr. Reed said, and looked genuinely perplexed.

"Maybe her water heater didn't quit working till this afternoon," I offered.

Bertha gave me an annoyed stare.

Chapter 2

On a peaceful afternoon three days later, Cara, another of my associate workers, and an uncommunicative girl with flat brown hair and an acne-scarred complexion, stuck her head through the door of the lounge.

"Will you go out to the front of the store, Holly, while I get some more candy? I've got to get this special order out to Mrs. Ransdell right away."

"Sure. I was about finished with my break anyway."

"Mrs. Ransdell wants a two-pound box of chocolate-covered cashews, caramel biscuits, and coconut creams. Ain't that a wild combination?'' Then Cara darted through the door before I could give her an answer. But at least she *had* said a few words to me. That was more than she usually did.

I quickly drained the last of my Pepsi and walked back through the storeroom to the retail section of the shop. A young man was standing at the far end of the fountain when I arrrived. He was very handsome, with dark blond hair streaked lighter in places by the sun, and blue eyes that looked large and round in his tan face. His eyes were such a clear blue that I could distinguish their color all the way across the room. The young man smiled a beautiful snow-white smile as I approached the fountain, and I could see that he was better-than-average height for a man and had a broad, muscular build.

''I'm sorry I kept you waiting.''

''Oh, that's okay. I just got here anyway.'' His voiced flowed smoothly from his lips, like a quiet stream beside a grassy hillside.

''What would you like?''

''I'll have a hot fudge sundae—with extra fudge.''

I reached for a silver dish lined with white paper, then nestled two scoops of vanilla ice cream, one on top of the other, and picked up the laddle of the hot fudge container. I turned to the young man. ''I'll have to charge you for the extra fudge.''

He offered me his smile again. It was bright and happy like sunshine. ''I know.''

In a minute I set the sundae and a glass of water in front of him on the black marble counter. ''That'll be 85 cents, please.''

He dug into a pocket of his trousers, and that was when I noticed the aluminum forearm crutches propped beside him against the fountain. I stared at them for only a minute, but the young man looked up suddenly, catching my gaze. Our eyes locked and held, and I tried to say or do something that would keep him from feeling uncomfortable. But he seemed to sense my problem, for his quiet expression told me that I need not be concerned.

He laid some change on the counter and singled out three quarters and a dime. I raked them into my hand. "Thank you."

"You're welcome."

I turned and deposited the money in the cash register.

"You're new here," he said to the back of my head.

I came around to face him. "I took Beverly's place."

"Has she had her baby yet?"

"She has another month to go."

"I guess it's pretty hard for a pregnant woman to stand on her feet a lot."

His soft-voiced reply took me by surprise. I nodded my agreement and stood gaping like a fool at his attractive features. He really was one of the finest-looking young men I had ever seen, certainly just as handsome as Steve.

"Don't you want to sit down?" I asked at length.

He looked up from his sundae. "I tried it once, but it's kind of tricky trying to balance myself on one of these high stools in this suit of armor."

I knew I gave him a puzzled look because then he said, "My braces, that's what I call them—my suit of armor." He glanced sideways, continuing. "They sort of go along with the crutches."

He spoke with such sweetness and laughter in his voice that I couldn't help smiling. "I've never met a real knight in shining armor before."

He flushed slightly. "Maybe you haven't yet, just a fool in leather and steel."

We both laughed and I saw it again—his springtime smile of sunshine. Suddenly I remembered the conversation I'd had a few days before with Bertha and Linda Benton. It was about the Britton brothers, sons of the local banker. One was a dark, suave ladies' man; the other one was fair, good-looking, and nice—and he was crippled. If I was talking to one of the Britton brothers, there could be no doubt about which one it was.

"You don't have to sit on the fountain," I said. "You can sit at one of the tables."

"Sometimes I do, but I'd just as soon stand here right now if I don't bother you."

"Oh, no, you don't bother me."

He took a bite of his ice cream. When it was gone he said, "Are you helping Mr. Reed with the office work like Beverly did or do you just work out here on the fountain?"

"I work out here in the afternoons. In the mornings I work in the office."

"I think Mr. Reed likes that arrangement. He's not fond of paperwork. He likes to be out here with the customers."

I nodded my agreement.

"Are you learning to work in the candy, too?"

"No, not yet. Mr. Reed said sometime later on he might let Cara or Bertha teach me. That's quite something, knowing how to recognize all those different pieces of chocolates just by the way they look. I think it's kind of wonderful that Mr. Reed still hand-dips all his own chocolates. I suppose his homemade candy is the best in this town."

"This is some kind of beautiful place to work in, isn't it?"

I glanced slowly around the long, high-ceilinged room of the shop, taking in the rich decor of mahogany woodwork set against the shine of mirrored walls and the sparkle of glass cases. "I've never seen anything like it."

"This place has real class. I'll bet there's not another shop like this one anywhere around here." He spooned more of his sundae. "Where's Bertha today?"

"She's delivering candy orders for Mr. Reed. We're pretty swamped with orders for Mother's Day."

Just then one of the rear doors opened and Cara came in, the front of her pale-green uniform hidden from view by a tall stack of white boxes.

My customer turned his dark-blond head, then threw up one arm. "Hi, Hardwork, I was just about to ask where you were."

Cara set the boxes on the counter by the telephone. "Hi, when'd you get back?"

"Yesterday. I missed you."

Cara blushed a strong shade of red and for the first time I saw a hint of a smile on her blemished face.

"Where've you been?" I quietly inquired of the young man.

"Florida. My grandparents have a house at Fort Myers Beach. I usually go down and stay for a few weeks every year."

"I've been to Fort Lauderdale. I really like the beach."

"Do you like to sail?"

"I don't know; I've never tried it."

He finished his hot fudge in silence. "I think I'll have a Coke," he said. "A large one."

I filled a tall glass and set it before him. He gave me 50 cents and I put it in the cash register.

"May I ask your name?" he said.

I came back to the end of the fountain. "It's Holly English."

"I'm Leroy Britton," he said, smiling his sunny smile again and offering me a steady hand. "I work at the bank around the corner."

We shook hands and I was taken by surprise at the tremendous strength in his fingers. But it felt good, and as we stood there smiling, hands clasped, I studied the prominent, determined line of his jaw and the contrasting gentle curve of his mouth. He looked like a person who would succeed at whatever he set out to do in life, and I could tell that he was of a refined, courteous nature, not at all rough or harsh.

"Leroy, that's a Latin name. It means 'royal.' "

"How do you know that?"

"I like to study names and where they come from. It's sort of a hobby. 'Royal' suits you, I think, a kind of 'Royal Knight.' "

"Suit of armor and all." Leroy tossed his head back and laughed. "What does Holly mean?" he asked in a minute.

"It means 'good luck.' It's an Anglo-Saxon name."

"Has it brought you good luck?"

"I don't know. I'm not sure if I really believe in such things."

"I know what you mean." He took a lingering drink of his Coke. "Is Mr. Reed making candy or ice cream today?"

"He's way in the back in the kitchen making candy."

"He's usually out here bending my ear when he's not busy." He drained his glass. "Have you been into the candy yet?"

I nodded. "It's pretty hard to resist Mr. Reed's peanut butter cups. But he said it was okay. He said we can eat all the candy we want."

"Just be careful you don't get fat like Bertha."

"Don't you like fat women?"

His clear, blue gaze traced the crack in the marble near the end of the fountain. "Oh, I...uh..."

"I just thought you might have a preference," I said, trying to help his obvious embarrassment and feeling sorry for my quick words. But that's usually how it was with me. I'd speak too soon, or too emphatically, and then wish I hadn't.

"I like them...not too fat," he finally said, taking up his crutches.

"I'll be seeing you," I called as he started toward the door.

He stopped in the middle of the floor and turned his head

and shoulders. "It was nice meeting you, Holly."

"Same here."

He glanced at Cara. "So long, Hardwork."

She looked up from the box of candy she was packing and smiled slowly. " 'Bye, Leroy."

I watched Leroy Britton swing his legs out the door and onto the sidewalk. He seemed like such a fine young man. What a shame it was for him, I thought, that he was crippled.

When Bertha returned from making candy deliveries, it was almost time to go home. "You going home to your cat?" she said as we collected our purses and prepared to leave.

I nodded and we started out. Immediately Bertha dug into her purse for a cigarette. She lit it up and took a long draw. When she let it out, smoke billowed in the warm air.

"I like you, Holly, but you're an odd one like Cara, ain't you?"

"Why do you say that?"

"Living by yourself and taking in stray cats and giving them far-out names."

"Does Cara do that?"

"No, but she's strange in other ways. She's hard to get to know and it's hard to like someone you can't know."

"I don't live by myself entirely by choice," I said bluntly.

"Oh, I didn't mean it that way. I know you said your parents are dead, but you could get a roommate like I did when I moved out of my parents' house."

"And I happen to like cats," I went on. "They're intelligent...well, for animals they are."

We stood outside on the sidewalk and I examined Bertha thoughtfully. I tried to find something likable about Bertha, for I was sure she had some pleasing qualities. Her name meant "shiny" or "bright." I moved on quickly. It appeared that

Bertha had a long way to go to live up to her name.

"Do you really think I'm strange?"

"Not strange, just a little different."

"Different? How? Living alone with a pet isn't really all that odd. A lot of people do it."

"You never go when I ask you to go with my roommate and me to that nice little singles bar a few blocks over and have a drink after work. Holly, you could be sociable."

"I *am* sociable, but I don't drink alcoholic beverages."

"Then you could order a Coke."

Yes, I could, I thought, but I still didn't think I'd care for the atmosphere. All that smoke and loud music. But how could I say that to Bertha without sounding pious and goody-goody? I chose to respond to what she had said earlier. "And about living alone, it's not bad. I like some privacy and it's better for something I like to do a lot."

Bertha grinned curiously. "And what is it, Holly English, that you like to do alone a lot?"

"Well, it's not much more than a hobby so far, but...I like to write."

"Write? Oh, Holly, you are a peculiar bird!" She peered strangely at me from her dark, expressive eyes. "I get a feeling you hear a different drummer than most of us."

I held Bertha's gaze for along moment, thinking I'd at last found one nice quality about her. She did have lovely eyes, so rich and full of meaning and expression. "Maybe I just believe there's more than one tune to be played."

Bertha shrugged.

"Could be, but whatever it is, we'll have to figure it out later. I've got to run now or I'll miss my ride. Tell Chow Mein hello and I'll see you tomorrow."

"Okay. 'Bye." I watched Bertha hurriedly carry her ample

figure up the sidewalk. Then I started across the street to the bus stop and thought about what Bertha had said. She had perceived a difference in me. I wondered if she would understand when I told her what that difference was.

Chapter 3

❧❧❧

The next day, during the early afternoon, I heard the door of the shop open, and casually glanced up from making a fresh pot of coffee. Another fine-looking young man came inside. He was slightly taller and much leaner than Leroy and as dark as Leroy was fair, with gently waving black hair and enormous dark-brown eyes. But I saw a distinct resemblance in the same determined line of his jaw and contrasting gentle curve of his mouth. The resemblance ended there, however, for the young man sauntered over to the fountain with an overstated, arrogant grace and plopped onto a stool directly in front of me.

"Whatta ya' say, beautiful!"

"Hello. What would you like?"

"You must be Holly."

I nodded.

"Mr. Reed's getting better taste in his old age. You're sure an improvement over the others."

I didn't like his aggressive remark, but I let it pass. "What would you like?"

He ran his dark-brown eyes unashamedly over my small, slender body. "How about a date?"

I flung the young man an angry glance. If he was the other banker's son that Bertha and Linda Benton had told me about, I decided that their idea of an interesting and exciting young man was vastly different from mine.

Different. That was how Bertha had described me. Maybe her description was more fitting than I realized. "Do you always come on like this?"

"I don't believe in wasting time."

"Well, you can just back off."

His smooth lips curved into a hint of a smile and his dark eyes mocked and laughed at me. "I like you, Holly—you've got spirit."

I sensed that what he said was his idea of a compliment. "Thank you. Now what may I get you?"

"Oh, I'll have my usual."

"I'm sorry. What would your 'usual' be?"

"You mean you don't know?" he asked as though I should trip and fall on my ignorance. "Haven't the other girls told you?"

I shook my head.

"I don't suppose you know who I am either?"

Oh, brother! "Guilty as charged."

My fine-looking customer drew up straight on his stool like a giant eagle about to spread his impressive wings. "Why, I'm Michael Britton!"

It wasn't a statement. It wasn't even an announcement. It was more of a noble proclamation. I couldn't tolerate it. "Oh... you're Leroy's brother."

His expression of glory faded. "Yeah, well, it's too bad about Leroy, but we can't all be tall, dark, and handsome."

This was *too* much. "Well, how about big, blond, and beautiful?"

Michael paled. "Huh?"

"Leroy."

"Sure thing," he mumbled, coming to his feet.

"Don't you want some ice cream?" I called as he shrank across the floor like an injured dog crawling off to lick his wounds.

"No," he returned over his shoulder, "I have to get back to work."

The door jingled open and I smile mischievously as he vanished into the street. I stood there a minute, thinking back over my repertoire of names and origins. Michael was a Hebrew name; it meant "Godlike." I shuddered. A mistake had surely been made somewhere. Michael Britton was anything but Godlike.

I didn't see Michael for a while after that, but Leroy came in the shop nearly every afternoon. He always stood at the end of the fountain eating hot fudge sundaes, with extra fudge, and smiling and being so nice. It was almost closing time about a week after I had met Leroy when the door of the shop opened and he swung himself inside. He called a greeting to Bertha and Cara, who were filling last-minute orders behind a candy case, then made his way over to the fountain.

"Hello, Ms. Good Luck."

"A hot fudge sundae will spoil your dinner."

He began his springtime grin. "I'll just have a Coke."

When I set it on the counter, he propped his crutches against the fountain and dug in his pocket for some change. He gave me the correct amount and I put it in the cash register. Then I busied myself wiping the fountain shining clean. This was one of Mr. Reed's top priorities. He staunchly believed that cleanliness was next to godliness, and so a specific time was set aside each week for nothing but cleaning the fountain. It was a mandate, and everyone joined in cheerfully, making the task move along quite pleasantly and rapidly.

Before long I heard Mr. Reed's lively steps coming from his office. His lanky frame appeared in one of the back doors, and then he came up behind the fountain. Such a compliant soul, Mr. Reed was easy to get to know, and everyone in the neighborhood, from shoe salesman to banker's son, liked to come to the candy shop for rich refreshment and long conversation.

"Leroy! I heard you were back. How was your trip, boy?"

"Just great, sir. You really should take some time off and go down there."

Mr. Reed took a key from the cash register drawer, then went around to the front door as Cara and Bertha came out from behind the candy cases and said good night. He locked the door after them.

"I've been giving it some serious thought," the elderly man said when he returned to the fountain. "Abigail Haysley goes to Orlando in the winter. She seems to think I'd like it."

I smiled to myself while listening to Leroy and Mr. Reed. Too bad Bertha had missed it all. She would have delighted in Mr. Reed's account of Abigail Haysley's ploy to get him down South next winter.

"Florida's a wonderful place to relax," said Leroy.

"That suntan looks good on you, boy."

"I spent most of my time out on the water."

"In that sailboat of yours?"

"Yes, sir." Leroy set his glass on the counter and glanced at me. "Well, I guess I'd better be going."

I had caught the reluctant look in his eyes, but I didn't think Mr. Reed had. I was wrong.

"Hadn't you better be getting home too, Holly?" said my employer.

"Yes, sir," I replied, noting the merriment in his jolly gray eyes. I took my purse from a drawer under the counter, and Mr. Reed escorted Leroy and me to the door.

Out on the sidewalk we stood facing each other. "Do you have a way home?" he asked in a minute.

"I was going to catch the bus."

"My car's just around the corner in the bank's parking lot. I could take you home...that is, if you want me to."

"You drive?" I asked bluntly. It was a stupid and inconsiderate remark.

Of course Leroy could drive if he had a car and was offering to take me home. Me and my big mouth! I was sure I had hurt his feelings. If only I could learn to think before I spoke. But Leroy seemed to understand.

"My car is equipped with hand controls," he said quietly, as though it was an explanation he'd had to offer more than once.

"Oh...well, I think it would be very kind of you to take me home."

Just then I spied a heavyset man with graying hair threading his way hurriedly through the traffic. I recognized him as

Mr. Wingfield, owner of the rambling, three-story department store across the street.

"Leroy, am I glad I caught you!" He glanced at me with a sigh of relief, then nodded agreeably before going on. "That nitwit brother of yours got our account fouled up while you were gone on vacation. He hired a new girl to run one of the computers and she didn't know what she was doing. I've never seen such a mess! Do you think you could have someone look into it?"

"I'd be glad to, sir, and I'm sorry about the trouble."

"I started to go to your dad, but I know he's a busy man. I knew if I could just hang in there till you got back I could rely on you to take care of it. I would've been over to see you already, but I thought you were going to be gone another week."

"Dad would have been glad to look into it, Mr. Wingfield."

"I know he would, Leroy, but I didn't want to say anything. You know what I mean?"

Leroy nodded, a look of unpleasant resignation on his face.

"Well, I've got to get home; my wife's expecting me early tonight. We're supposed to go to some fool dinner party. I happened to see you as I was leaving and I wanted to mention the account to you. It sure is nice to know there's someone like you I can depend on." He started back across the street.

"See you later, Mr. Wingfield," Leroy called, "and don't worry about your account. I'll see that someone takes care of it."

Leroy and I went up the sidewalk and around the corner to the bank, past the rear of the building to a new white Buick. After Leroy opened the door for me, he went around to the other side and let himself in. He slid his crutches on the back floor and sank into the seat. I watched him take his hands and lift each one of his legs and place them heavily beneath the steering wheel. I wondered what it could possibly be like to not have any feeling in your lower limbs and to have them bound in long, cumbersome braces and have to maneuver them the way Leroy did. I tried to imagine it but could not.

After Leroy had closed the door and started the car, he worked some levers mounted on the steering post, and soon we left the parking lot and flowed into the stream of traffic.

"Where do you live?" he asked as we went along.

"On Hillshire Drive."

"I guess I should've asked you before, and now here I am taking you home. What if you did have a husband waiting for you?"

"I don't, but it would be okay if I did."

"I didn't think you were married, you've never mentioned it and you don't wear a ring, but if you have a husband I just thought he might not like for me to bring you home."

"He wouldn't mind."

"I suppose not."

I looked over at Leroy. There was something in the tone of his voice. It was so sad. "Why did you say it like that?"

He cast me a quick glance. His eyes plainly spoke the words his lips didn't say, and I knew exactly what he was thinking. I could read his face so clearly that it was almost as though I could read his mind as well. My heart ached for Leroy as I suddenly realized how inadequate he must feel in some ways because of his disability. I sought to reassure him that his handicap didn't hinder our relationship.

"What I meant was, I'd never marry a man who'd get angry just because a friend brought me home from work."

Leroy didn't offer any response. He just kept his eyes steadied on the road ahead. We rode in silence and I sat beside him feeling sorry and foolish for all my thoughtless comments.

"I didn't mean anything *else*," I finally said. "Oh, I'm sorry!"

He glanced quickly at me then, and a sudden light that gleamed in his blue eyes told me that he understood. "Then your boyfriend won't object if I take you home, will he?" he said shortly.

"No." Then unexpectedly Steve crossed my mind. But of course *he* wouldn't mind. He'd be glad, especially now.

"You're sure? I couldn't do much about it if he wanted to punch me in the nose."

He glanced at me again and I caught a glimpse of sunshine. I flashed a smile back, glad that he had picked up the conversation.

"So you're a coward, huh?"

"No, just a little limited in what I can do."

"I don't have a boyfriend." I thought Leroy might smile again, but he didn't.

Instead, he looked frightfully earnest and said, "Do you live with your parents?"

"My parents are dead. My mother died when I was little and my father was killed in a plane crash two years ago."

"I'm sorry," he said, his calm blue eyes wide with sincerity as they focused on me again.

"I've pretty well adjusted to it. I can barely remember my mother, but my father and I were very close. He was really a grand ol' guy."

"Do you have any brothers and sisters?"

"No."

"Didn't your father ever remarry?"

"He had a thing about marriage and about my mother. He said that the Bible says one woman for one man for a lifetime."

"I don't think the Bible meant for a man to feel that way if death parted him from his wife."

I gazed uncertainly at Leroy. It had been a long time since a young man had spoken to me of the Bible, except for Steve, of course. He was so spiritually strong and had helped me much in my spiritual growth. Sometimes we had spent hours with the Scriptures, reading them to each other and discussing what they meant and praying over them.

"I think what my father was really trying to say was that my mother was the only woman for him forever."

Leroy seemed to be considering what I said, and I wondered what he thought of that kind of faithfulness, if he admired it in the light of traditional Biblical values or considered it unwarranted in the view of current declining standards.

"Some men are like that, you know."

"It's good to know they are. I'm sure your father's choice was the right one for him."

"I can see that it wouldn't be right for everyone. I'm sure even my father was very lonely at times, even though he and I had such a close association."

"Loneliness can be a steady battle," Leroy said. From the melancholy tone in his voice, I was positive that he wasn't referring to my father. "Don't you have any family here now?"

"Oh, sure, my church family, which in some ways is my truest family because we're the sons and daughters of God."

Leroy cast a brief look in my direction. It seemed that I saw a questioning gaze in his clear eyes, but when he didn't say anything I went on. "I suppose you meant my flesh-and-blood family. No, they aren't here. My mother's family lives in California and my father's people are in England, except for one sister. She lives in Virginia, but we keep in contact."

"Well, you have close friends here?"

Steve was the first one who came to mind, but I dismissed him immediately. "Old friends from school, of course, but most of them are married and have their own lives now. My closest friends are my friends at church. We do almost everything together, like shopping and going to movies and plays and to dinner."

We turned off the main street then, and I asked Leroy about his work at the bank.

"I work in the loan department."

"You're being modest. Linda Benton said you were her boss—a vice-president, she said. Being in charge of the loan department must carry tremendous responsibility."

"I make a lot of decisions, but it's all in a day's work."

"Does you father actually own the bank?"

"Yes, we're a private bank; there are very few of those in operation today. Most banks are capital stock. They're owned by stockholders who paid money to help get the bank started and keep it running.

"Dad's brother owns part of our bank, and Michael and I have part. Dad's portion, the largest, will be divided between Michael and me someday."

"Does Michael do anything?" I blurted out, then stole a prudent glance at Leroy. He seemed to be trying to suppress a grin. "I mean from what Mr. Wingfield said a while ago. Oh, I mean, well...what does Michael do?"

Leroy let the grin work its way into his face. "You don't like Michael very much, do you?"

"Well, I know I shouldn't say so, but I really don't like his aggressive attitude. It definitely takes away from his...charm."

Leroy looked over at me, then threw his head back and laughed. In a minute he said, "What did you do to him the other day? He came back to the bank looking like a deflated balloon. When I asked him what was wrong, he said something about the dumb broad at the candy store.''

Leroy laughed again and I couldn't help smiling with him.

"I thought he must be talking about you because Cara doesn't say anything to him and Bertha falls all over him every time he goes in there.''

"Maybe I was a little unkind to him," I said somewhat apologetically, although I didn't feel any regrets for my words to Leroy's brother. Somewhere in this world there had to be a *little* justice.

"Michael isn't used to getting put down, especially by a woman.''

"It won't hurt him to walk in your shadow for a while— you've probably walked in his for a long time.''

Leroy looked puzzled and then suddenly uncomfortable when I told him what I had said to Michael.

"Michael's a vice-president too. He oversees the accounting department,'' Leroy said when he seemed to have recovered from my outspoken description of his physical attributes.

I checked a grin and wondered what he thought of my term— big, blond, and beautiful. Thinking it over, it sounded like a bold and unladylike statement. I glanced at Leroy, hoping he didn't think I was that kind of young woman. "I can't imagine Michael being in charge of anything, especially accounting.''

"He does better than you think. He has to or dad wouldn't have him around.''

"I guess having him in the accounting department is better than having him make loans.''

Leroy chuckled. "Once in a while he gets a little slack. Michael has the ability—he was educated in business and finance and economics, and he has a college degree the same as I do. But sometimes he doesn't like to apply himself as an administrator.''

"Like with Mr. Wingfield's account?"

Leroy nodded. "Michael hired a beautiful girl to run that computer. She probably looked so good to him that he didn't care about her qualifications."

"I sensed a little resentment in Michael the other day—toward you, I mean. Is he jealous of you because you're better at your job than he is?"

"I'm not better at my job, not when Michael applies himself, but he wouldn't be jealous of that anyway. He doesn't care. He's more interested in having a good time right now."

"But I did feel something the other day."

"Oh, Michael just clowns around a lot. I wouldn't pay any attention to him."

Though Leroy sounded sincere, I distinctly felt that he was trying to smooth over Michael's attitude or cover it up in some way.

"Are you older than Michael?"

"I'm 27 and he's 24, which may account for why he's still sowing a few wild oats."

"And what about you?"

"Me?"

"Are you still sowing your wild oats?"

Leroy looked completely embarrassed. His face reddened and he drew in a long deep breath and stammered, "Oh...I...uh..."

I couldn't help laughing when he glanced over at me with the most helpless and forlorn expression on his handsome face.

"I'm sorry," I told him. "It seems like I say all the wrong things to you."

"It's okay." He paused a minute as if to collect his thoughts. "I guess I'm not the swinging type like Michael."

"I'm glad you're not, but I find it hard to believe that someone isn't taking up your time."

Leroy looked at me with the sweetest expression in his clear blue eyes. "I guess I'm sort of unoccupied right now."

When we got to the street where I lived, I directed Leroy to the first apartment complex on the left. "I live in the back, number 1604."

He pulled into a parking space in front of the white brick building with black wooden shutters and stared at the car parked beside us. "That's a good-looking thing, isn't it?"

"It's a Saab Sonett III. They're made in Sweden."

He looked at me in mild wonder. "Is it yours?"

"My father gave it to me just before he died. I don't drive it to work, though. I only live a half-block from the bus line. That's more convenient. I don't have to fight traffic and bother with parking, not to mention buying gas."

"I think you're doing the smart thing." He reached for the door handle. "If you'll give me a minute, I'll come around and open the door for you."

When Leroy had placed his legs firmly outside on the smooth surface of the street, he retrieved his cruthces from the floor of the back seat and soon he was at my door opening it wide. We went up the walk together.

"These are nice apartments," he said, glancing around at the neat lawns of occasional flowers and well-kept shrubbery. "Have you lived here very long?"

"I moved here not long after my father died. I just had to get out of our big, empty house—you know what I mean?"

He nodded. "There are some other real nice apartments not too far from here, over on Rollingford."

"Have you been looking at them?"

"Yes, I've been thinking about getting my own place."

We reached my door then, and Leroy stood looking down at me like a little lost puppy dog.

"Won't you come in?" I said. "I'll make us a bite to eat if you're not in a hurry."

He hesitated a fleeting moment. "I can't tonight, but thanks anyway."

"Are you sure? It won't take me very long. I'm not much of a cook, but I'll throw something together."

"I'm sorry, I really can't," he said, and his voice was so warm and sweet. "I have to go to a meeting and I don't know how long I'll be. A group of us have begun meeting about some proposals we want to get before the Board of Aldermen, who are helping to fund our organization."

"What kind of porposals?"

"Our group is called HAL—for Handicapped Action League. We're hoping to bring about more public awareness for some needed inprovements in public accommodations for disabled people—ramps and automatic doors for wheelchairs and other things like that which will make places of business more accessible to the physically disabled."

"I suppose those of us who don't have any physical limitations take so much for granted. We don't think of what a person in a wheelchair or on crutches might be going through."

"I don't think it's a case of deliberate neglect on the part of the majority," Leroy said with obvious concern. "But disabled persons have been terribly discriminated against in this area for so long."

"I'm sure your group will do the proper things needed to bring about these improvements, and I hope they come about very soon."

"We're pretty confident. We've been meeting with some of the local businessmen. At first there was some cost opposition, but most of them are more than willing to cooperate and make changes. They just haven't thought of doing them. It isn't hard to see that if more places of business are accessible to the disabled, they're naturally going to patronize these places and that will mean more retail business."

I gazed up at Leroy as he spoke, studying the calm blue of his eyes and the gentle curve of his mouth. He seemed to have many of the qualities that I admired in a man. He was intelligent and friendly and humorous, but most of all he was kind and sweet. There couldn't be any doubt about his integrity, either, and he even seemed to know something about the Bible. This made me want to get to know him better.

"Can you come back after your meeting? I'll keep something warm."

"No...no, I can't, thanks."

I sensed a reluctance in Leroy that I didn't understand. I could tell he really wanted to come back, but something held his feelings in check. Perhaps it was the inadequacy that I had detected in him earlier. Perhaps he was a little unsure of himself when it came to a more personal relationship with a woman.

"You have to eat sometime," I persisted.

"I'll grab a bite at the drugstore. Thanks anyway."

Our conversation lapsed into silence and we just stood staring at each other.

"I suppose I'd better be letting you go to your meeting," I said at last. "You were very kind to bring me home. Thank you."

"It was a pleasure."

Chapter 4

In the week that followed, Leroy came to the candy shop every afternoon. As was his custom, he stood at the end of the fountain eating hot fudge sundaes and drinking Cokes and talking to me when I wasn't busy. We began to get better acquainted this way and I came to like him very well. I knew how much he liked me, too, because Bertha kept commenting about how Leroy had never been such a steady customer at the shop before coming back from his Florida vacation and finding me behind the fountain.

"Oh, he's always come in here a lot," Bertha said. "He and

ol' Mr. Reed always got something to jaw about, but the main reason he comes in here now is to see you, Holly.''

It was Monday afternoon and I was helping Cara change the Mother's Day displays in the front windows of the shop when the door chimed open. I looked up from a colorful tin packed with fruits and nuts. Michael came strutting inside like a peacock wearing recycled feathers. It was easy to see how his dark good looks could turn a young woman's head. He really was an attractive man. What a pity that he didn't have a personality to match, I thought.

Michael swaggered over to where Bertha stood behind a tall, slender jar of candy canes. She was grouping fresh flowers to add to the new displays.

"Whatta ya' say, baby?"

"Oh, hi, Michael," she cooed.

"Was that *you* I saw out with Burt Reynolds last night?" Bertha giggled foolishly.

"You better cool it with those Hollywood dudes. I don't like them beating my time."

"Oh, Michael, you're such a tease!"

The handsome young banker's son laughed loudly. Too loudly, I thought. It sounded phony and pretentious.

He strolled across the floor and took a seat on one of the red leather stools at the fountain. I left the window display and came around to wait on him.

"Fix me a pineapple malt, will you, baby? And make it extra thick."

I nodded and moved promptly away. I could feel Michael's gaze as I worked, his dark eyes penetrating, boring smoldering holes through my pale green uniform. I filled a malt can with three scoops of vanilla ice cream, then added some milk, a squirt of pineapple syrup, and a dash of malt. A few minutes later

I set a tall glass of thick, yellow liquid before him. He gave me a single bill, and I put it in the cash register and returned with his change.

"I don't blame my brother for beating it down here every day," Michael said. "You look real good standing back there."

"I'm assuming you mean that as a compliment, so I'll say thank you."

"Are you kidding? I think you're one of the greatest-looking babes I've ever seen. All that beautiful black hair and those big green eyes and that cute little figure. You can't miss, baby."

I appreciated Michael's praise, but I didn't take him seriously. I knew his type well. Like all of them, he was too quick and aggressive with his comments.

He took a drink from his malt. "You oughta see ol' Leroy flying out of the bank to come down here." He chuckled. "You oughta watch ol' Leroy going down the street. One of these days his crutches are going to slip out from under him and he'll fall flat."

I glared hard at Michael, and I knew my whole face was covered with astonishment. "You're a very cruel man, Mr. Britton!" I picked up a jar of strawberry syrup and bent to place it under the counter for storage. I had to do something, so extreme was the degree of my anger. I even considered tossing the jar at Michael Britton.

My thoughts must have been visible in my face, for then Michael said, "Hey, I was only kidding."

"Do you always make jokes at your brother's expense?"

"Ol' Leroy doesn't care."

I didn't make any reply. I didn't have anything more to say to Michael Britton. But I stood there remembering what Mr. Reed had told me about being nice to the customers—that in selling a product to the public, if you had to make a choice between a bad product and a bad disposition, a bad disposition was by far the worst. I thought back over the scene with Michael and I knew our product wasn't bad; that left only my disposition.

"Are you from around here?" Michael asked.

"Yes, I am."

"How come I've never seen you?"

"I don't know."

"I must be going to all the wrong places."

"You could be—it's a pretty big town."

A mischievous gleam danced in Michael's dark-brown eyes. "Why don't you go to some of those places with me?"

I glanced across the store at Bertha. I knew she had been listening to my conversation with Michael, and I wondered what kind of reaction she had to his question. She had left her flower arrangements behind the slender jar of candy canes and had moved to a plump jar of licorice buttons. She stood peering over the lid, watching us furtively and chomping anxiously on a mouthful.

I looked toward the front of the shop at the big windows on each side of the broad old door. Cara had climed into one of the windows and was working on one of the new displays by herself.

Maybe I was using Cara as an excuse to delay a confrontation with Michael, but the girl suddenly struck me as I watched her work. I quickly summoned my memory of names and their origins and groped about for Cara's. Not a common name, hers was of Celtic origin, a subfamily of languages including Gaelic and Welsh. I thought Cara meant "friend." It occured to me then what a loner she was and I wondered if perhaps she could use a friend. I resolved to make an effort to be more communicative with her in the future.

"Well, why don't you go out with me, baby?" Michael was saying.

"No, thank you."

"You mean you're turning down a chance to go out with Michael Britton?"

"Is that so hard to believe?"

"Nobody will believe it."

I smiled whimsically at his pompous arrogance, ashamed to admit that hidden beneath his overstated grace there did appear to be a certain small amount of stale charm. "How many people are you going to tell?"

"Not many—a thing like this could ruin my reputation."

"I doubt if anything could do that."

A passive grin parted Michael's smooth lips. "I think you're putting me on, Holly. Don't you know that playing hard-to-get went out with ducktail haircuts?"

"I'm not playing hard-to-get—I'm just not interested."

"Oh, I suppose you're interested in Leroy." He laughed. It was loud and showy. "Why would a girl like you be interested in Leroy?"

"Just what kind of girl should be interested in him?"

Michael glanced toward the front of the store. "Cara's more Leroy's type," he said in a lowered voice, "not a babe like you. So why the interest?"

"I never said I was interested in Leroy—you did—but if I were I don't think you'd understand."

"Try me."

I shook my head.

"Oh, come on."

I thought about Michael's brother for a minute—his soft voice and gentle ways, his clear eyes and bright smile. "He's sunshine."

Michael howled with laughter. I knew he would. He picked up his malt glass. "You really like him?"

"Yes, I do."

"What are you, some kind of weirdo?"

"I don't know what you mean."

Michael drained his glass and returned it to the counter. Then he stood up and leaned over the fountain. "Come on, baby, you're too good to waste on a guy like my brother. He probably doesn't even know what to do with a woman like you. Whatta ya say we go out to the lake tonight and—"

"Forget it, Michael, you're way out of your league."

He gathered himself up. "I thought I rated around here, but I can see I'm not very important to you."

"My father used to say if you want to know how important you are, just stick your finger down in a bucket of water and the size of the hole you leave when you take your finger out will show how important you are."

Michael laughed again. It wasn't a funny laugh this time, and not loud either—just an exaggerated ripple, a sort of chuckle to hide in. He left the fountain and sauntered defiantly across the floor. "Okay, I know when I've been had." At the door he paused and turned back in my direction. "When you get tired of 'the cripple' and want a real man, look me up!"

Following Michael's haughty departure, Bertha rushed her ample frame over the the fountain. "Holly, have you lost your mind?"

"I don't think so."

"Michael Britton just asked you to go out and you turned him down!"

"Really, he's not my type."

"What is your type—Leroy?"

It was the way she said it that made me angry, so

mocking and critical. "What if he is?"

"I said you were different! At least I like normal men instead of—"

"You call Michael Britton normal? That egotistical, overbearing, obnoxious—"

"He's not crippled."

"I wouldn't count on it. I doubt if anyone's ever examined his brain—if he has one."

Bertha scanned my face carefully. "Were you really serious about liking Leroy?"

"I like him, yes."

"Why would you pick someone like him?"

"I haven't *picked* him—he's not a piece of fruit hanging from a vine—but what if I did? What do you mean 'someone like him'? What's wrong with him?"

"He's crippled."

"I hadn't noticed."

Bertha gawked at me, quite taken aback, but she recovered quickly enough. "Nobody in their right mind would want a man like that."

"That's right, Bertha, he *is* a man, not a freak. Just because he had polio and it left his legs paralyzed, does that mean he's devoid of all feeling?"

"Oh, brother, get you!"

"Leroy's kind and sweet and he's intelligent and fun."

"Sure he is, but he's still only half a man."

"That depends on what your measure of a man is. Mine doesn't have anything to do with how he gets around. I know Leroy's crippled, but it doesn't matter. He has so many fine qualities that his handicap fades in comparison. He has a lot more going for him than that shallow playboy you're so crazy about."

Bertha eyed me curiously. "I think Michael was right—you *are* weird." She shrugged. "If you get your kicks with Leroy's type, be my guest. If that's your thing—"

"It's not my *thing*. I don't know why you and that empty-headed Don Juan are making such a big deal of it. It's simple, really. When I look at Leroy, I don't see just a guy who once had a rotten disease. I see a warm and beautiful human being."

"Here we go again."

"I just don't know how Michael can talk about his brother the way he does," I went on. "It's so cruel and inconsiderate."

"Oh, don't be so sensitive. Michael makes jokes about Leroy all the time. He doesn't mean it. You know how brothers can be."

"No, I guess I don't know how brothers can be. But I think a little understanding and compassion would go a long way in helping Michael."

"Maybe so, but Leroy's still a cripple and I'd be ashamed to be seen walking down the street with him."

I picked up Michael's empty glass. "Maybe that's why you're always walking down the street by yourself!" I set the glass too hard in the metal sink. It broke. So did Bertha's proud expression.

At once I was sorry for my hasty words. Maybe Bertha was somewhat narrow-minded and insensitive in her thinking, but that still didn't give me any right to speak so sharply to her. But that was me, the outspoken Holly English, and I had hurt Bertha's feelings and maybe ruined any chance I might ever have to share my convictions with her. It seemed as though my hasty words were always getting me into trouble. How could I be the kind of Christian I should be if I couldn't control my tongue!

I laid my hand on Bertha's arm. "I'm sorry. I shouldn't have said that."

Her reaction took me by complete surprise. "Oh, that's okay. Maybe you're right anyway."

Chapter 5

My encounter with Bertha caused me to do some serious thinking. It seemed that sometimes my bold, plain-spoken ways made it easy for Satan to have his way with me. I knew I had to do something about that immediately, so I began to pray. Before long memories of the soul-winning class I had taken in church training came to mind. I thought of our pastor's wife, so peaceful, so assured, who had taught the class. Her soft-spoken words of truth echoed in the caverns of my mind: If you are to be a soul-winner, first be sure you are saved. (Of this I had no doubt.) Then, be filled with the Spirit. The Spirit causes us to nave compassion in our heart for all people, and He will burden our heart for lost persons. If we are burdened, we will do something about it. A person with compassion will be moved to action.

I recalled her teachings about the power of the Holy Spirit—how people are won through *Him*, not us. I remembered what I had been taught about the power of prayer, and I sent a prayer to heaven right then for Bertha, that I would have a chance to share my witness with her and that the Holy Spirit would prepare her heart to respond. Then I went over in my mind the power of the Word. I thought through Scriptures that pointed the way to salvation. I concluded by asking God to remove anything (such as my quick tongue) from my life that was keeping me from being used more fully by Him, anything in me that was preventing the Spirit from occupying every nook and cranny of my person. I asked for a thorough cleansing that I might be a proper vessel of His, and that everything I said and did would glorify Him.

The following day, at lunchtime, Bertha was in the lounge slumped in a chair reading a mystery novel and smoking a long cigarette.

"What is it with you and Leroy?" Bertha said suddenly. "I just don't understand you."

I had been mulling over exactly what Scripture I wanted to share with Bertha. My Bible was in my purse beside me on the table. I took it out. I knew by heart the passages I would use, but my witness would be more effective if I read some of them directly from the Word.

When Bertha mentioned Leroy's name, I paused, deciding I'd better clear that up first. "Bertha, about Leroy. I'm not...well, I'm not interested in him as you think.

We're just friends, new friends, that's all."

"Oh, that's okay, you don't have to explain to me. I could never go for a guy like that, but as they say—a difference of opinion is what makes a horse race."

Bertha's paltry remark put me on the defensive. "What if you cared for someone first and then an accident or disease crippled him—would you stop caring for him?"

"Well, no...oh, I don't know, but that's different."

"I don't see why." When Bertha didn't offer any further comment, I said, "I don't go for Leroy, not in the way you mean. I—" I stopped in time. I was about to say I go for Steve. But I couldn't tell Bertha about that. I couldn't tell anyone.

"You what?"

"I...just like Leroy for a friend." I turned back to my lunch, but I couldn't eat. I stared at my Bible.

"I like Leroy for a friend, too—everybody does. Poor ol' Leroy, he's everybody's friend but nobody's date."

I looked over at Bertha, wondering what she thought she was. To my knowledge she had never had a date in her life. But that was an unfair judgment of her. I hadn't known Bertha very long. Maybe it was something in the way she looked or acted. I suppose I just presumed that no one would want to take her out, at least not a refined and gracious young man like Leroy.

"Leroy takes girls out once in a while, I think," Bertha said. "Michael was telling us one time about a girl he took out from the bank. He thought the whole thing was pretty funny. She was a nice-looking girl, but one of those intellectual types. Michael said it was a good thing because Leroy probably didn't know how to do anything else but talk. He spends all his spare time on that boat of his, you know. I guess a hobby is all someone like—"

"I'm a Christian," I blurted out, interrupting Bertha's flow of empty chatter. "That's what's different about me." I was still looking at her because I wanted to see her response to what I'd said, but it wasn't necessary. She just laughed. It was like a loud hoot.

"Christians ain't any different from anybody else."

I must have looked surprised because she added, "Well, they're not."

"How do you mean, they're not any different?"

Bertha had finished her cigarette and paused to light another. She blew a huge puff of smoke in my direction. "Like smoking, for instance. When I ride the bus home from work, like when I stay and do some shopping or something and don't go with my ride, I pass this little church on the corner of Westwood and Ninth. They have church during the middle of the week, and I always see a bunch of men standing outside puffing away on their cigarettes. Even when it's cold, some of them are still there. I've always wondered why they come outside. Looks to me like if you're going to smoke, you're going to smoke. What difference does it make if it's inside or outside? If it's okay to do it, why not one place as well as another?"

"Maybe some Christians haven't seen that smoking dishonors God."

Bertha didn't look as though she understood what I said. "What are Christians supposed to do, go around with long faces and never have any fun? Don't they have any joy in life?"

"Oh, yes! Being a Christian is the greatest kind of joy! Jesus has paid our sin debt and we are assured of eternal life! Nothing is more wonderful than that!"

Bertha gazed at me as if she thought I'd suddenly separated from my sanity. Then she laughed her hooting laugh again. "You got it made, huh? So nothing else matters? You can do any old thing you want. It's okay for Christians but it's wrong for me!

"Is it any worse for a Christian to smoke than it is to blurt out things all the time and maybe hurt someone's feelings?"

Bertha appeared to vividly recall the time yesterday when I'd spoken so emphatically to her. "So what are you trying to say?"

"That Christians are human beings, and we're anything but perfect, but we've experienced God's grace of love and forgiveness and we want to share it with you if you'll let us...if you'll let me. I want to tell you what Jesus did for me and what a difference He makes in my life every day."

All this time Bertha had been puffing and puffing on her cigarette. She got up abruptly and snuffed out what was left of it. "I have to go back to work now. Save it for another time, okay?"

I sighed deep within as Bertha picked up her novel and hurried out of the lounge.

Chapter 6

At closing time the next Monday evening I had left the shop when I met Abigail Haysley charging up the sidewalk. Abigail was a Hebrew name. It meant "a source of joy." I wondered if she was a source of joy to Mr. Reed. Maybe. Probably.

"Oh, dear, am I too late?" asked Mrs. Haysley.

"I'm sorry, we just closed."

"But I must see Mr. Reed; I need his opinion on something very important."

A knowing smile parted my lips. "Well, why don't you go and knock on the door? He'll still be there for a few minutes. I'm sure he'll let you in."

She sprang forward like a spirited gazelle. "Yes, I'll do that. Thank you, dear."

I looked beyond Mrs. Haysley to see Leroy coming along the sidewalk. I moved to greet him.

He smiled and spoke with his usual regard: "Hello, Miss Good Luck."

"You're too late for a hot fudge sundae."

"I know. I've been unusually busy today, but I was hoping to catch you. Are you going home now? I could give you a ride."

"I have some shopping to do first."

"Oh." He gazed down at the concrete beneath our feet. I gazed up at him, studying his attractive features in the brilliant stream of light that poured over us from the late afternoon sun. I liked the way Leroy's dark blond hair highlighted so well in the bright rays of the sun, and it looked like it would be so soft to touch.

On impulse I said, "Why don't you come shopping with me?"

"Oh, I'd probably just get in your way."

"No, you wouldn't. I like having company when I shop."

He looked uncertainly at me. "You're probably going with some friends from your church."

Steve's face flashed across my mind, but of course I wouldn't be going shopping with him anymore. "No, I'm not." Then I added, "Come on, you can carry my packages."

I held my breath, hoping I hadn't said the wrong thing, that Leroy wouldn't think I was being flippant and cute. Then the soft grin on his tan face turned into a full-blown laugh and we started up the street. I glanced up at him out of the corner of my eye as we went along, deciding that Leroy was a kind of wonderful companion to have. Maybe he couldn't carry my packages, but I was perfectly capable of doing that myself, and he could do more important things. He was an excellent conversationalist and someone pleasing to be with. I felt good walking beside him. Unlike Bertha, I wasn't at all uncomfortable because of his disability; I only wished him better circumstances for his sake.

"As a matter of fact," Leroy was saying, "I need to get started with some shopping of my own. I rented one of those apartments on Rollingford that I mentioned to you, but I don't have much furniture yet, and I have to get linens and dishes and all those things."

"That'll be fun picking out all those household items. I had a great time when I furnished my apartment. I had some things I wanted to keep from the house, of course, but I had to get some new stuff, too. A lot of what we had in our house wouldn't go in my apartment."

Leroy looked over at me. In a minute he said, "Would you...that is, a woman's opinion would be good."

"Do you want me to look at some things with you?"

"You wouldn't mind?"

"I'd enjoy it."

"Maybe we can look at some things one night this week. I really need to be getting some stuff."

"Well, I can't tomorrow night. I volunteer at the information desk at the new hospital on Tuesday evenings, and then Wednesday's prayer meeting."

"Oh, well, that's all right. You're busy."

"We could look at some things tonight. It won't take long to get what I need."

"I suppose it's long past the time when I should have a place of my own. Michael got an apartment as soon as he finished college, but I stayed on with Mom and Dad when I finished. They seemed to like having someone back home again after a year with both Michael and me gone. I was in my last year when he began his freshman year."

"I don't know that there's any special time when a person should leave home—just when you feel it's right, I guess. Unless a person is getting married or something like that."

Leroy glanced briefly at me just then, and I got the unmistakable feeling that he thought getting married was the last thing he'd ever do.

"I hate to leave Mom and Dad's house in a way. It's out on Wyeth Lake, but it's really not that far to drive. Dad has always driven into the bank. But an apartment will be a nice change, and it's more practical now with the cost of operating a car going up, especially the jump in gasoline prices; it'll be good to be closer in town. And I can go out to the lake on weekends to sail.

"If I like apartment living, I may buy into a condo. Apartment rent is so high, especially when you consider you aren't getting any return on your investment."

"I've been giving that some thought too, but I want to go on renting awhile till I'm sure of what I want to do."

When I finished my shopping, Leroy and I had dinner at a little restuarant down the street from the bank. Then we went to Wingfield's Department Store, across from the candy shop, and picked out some items for his new apartment. It turned out that his taste in furnishings was quite good, and he seemed to have some definite ideas about what he wanted. He chose a mostly modern decor, not unlike my own, and he picked colors of my taste also—earth tones of brown and beige and rust. We hadn't been shopping very long when I discovered that Leroy had been doing some looking and comparing prior to making his final decisions, and it occurred to me that he needed a woman's opinion about as much as he needed three heads.

I smiled inwardly, wondering if he had asked me to come with him because he wanted my opinion or my company.

After Leroy made his purchases he drove me home. As we pulled up in front of my apartment building I reached into the back seat and picked up my few packages.

"I'm really sorry I can't help you take those in," he said.

I turned and looked deeply into his calm, blue eyes. For a minute I almost felt sorry for him. "Please, don't be sorry—it's okay."

He reached for his crutches on the back floor, then got out of the car and came around to open my door.

"You can do something else for me," I said when I stood facing him.

"Sure, what is it?"

"You can come in and talk to me while I put these things away." Before he could say no, I added, "Come on," and proceeded up the walk. I glanced back. He swung around and came after me.

I slowed till he caught up, and as we went along Leroy's presence seemed to loom great beside me. He was much taller than I was and his physique was quite overpowering in spite of the paralysis in his legs. He had such broad shoulders and very muscular arms and chest. I felt secure walking beside him like a maiden with her knight in shining armor, I thought.

I smiled up into his face, and when we neared the door the clinking sound that his steel braces made as he moved himself along echoed distinctly in my ears. I thought about the things Michael and Bertha had said and wondered if it really could be considered weird to be attracted to a man with a disability like Leroy's. I didn't wonder very long.

In my apartment Leroy settled down on the couch while I

took care of my packages. When I returned, he said, "Your place is real nice."

I glanced around the living room at the contemporary furniture, the walls covered with modern art, and the floor warmed with shaggy carpet. My gaze came to a stop at the glass-enclosed fireplace. "Thank you."

"I looked at some townhouses similar to these, but I decided on a one-floor apartment."

I lived in one of those townhouse complexes with two bedrooms (one which I used for an office) and a bath upstairs. An L-shaped living room and dining area made up the largest portion of the downstairs. Along a short hall was a guest bath and a washer/dryer unit. An open kitchen and den ran across the back of the apartment. French doors opened off the den onto a small patio.

"I kind of like having an upstairs. It seems more like a house, only not as big."

"Your cat sure is friendly," Leroy said, scratching my pale-eyed Siamese behind his darkly-tipped ears. "What's his name?"

"Chow Mein."

"Whatever made you give him a name like that?"

"You sound like Bertha," I laughed. "Anyway, one night I found him out behind these apartments. He was half-starved. The only thing I had here to eat was some leftover chow mein. He ate it up like it was the best meal he'd ever eaten. After that Chow Mein seemed like a natural thing to call him." I crossed the dining area to the kitchen and came back with two stemmed goblets that I placed on the glass coffee table in front of the couch. "Do you think these are too fancy for Pepsi?" I asked as Leroy scooted Chow Mein off his lap.

"No."

"My old maid aunt gave them to me—the one who lives in Virginia. She says it's elegant to serve your guests in these kind of glasses. I think she really had wine or something like that in mind."

I went to the kitchen again for a quart bottle of Pepsi, then sat down beside Leroy and poured the drink into the goblets. Out of the corner of my eye I saw Chow Mein disappear up the stairs. I knew where I would find him when it was time to get ready for bed. He would be curled up sound asleep right in the middle of my bed!

"I used to do this a lot when I was a little girl," I said. "I used to pretend I was well-to-do and very sophisticated, and I'd invite my pretend friends over and we'd drink from fancy glasses."

Leroy smiled, and for a moment I was lost in the glow of his handsome, tan features. His smile really was special—so bright, showing off his beautiful white teeth. While we quietly drank our Pepsi the tiniest feeling began to creep up and down the length of my spine.

Leroy's smooth voice broke into the stillness. "I guess growing up by yourself was lonely sometimes."

"Yes, it was sometimes, but I was pretty creative. I kept busy."

He nodded politely.

"How did everything go at your meeting last week?" I asked.

"You should have been there. We met at the bank, our facilities were being painted, and Michael just happened to drop by. It was really something to see the expression on his face when he opened the door of my office and there was a whole roomful of people like me. Some were on crutches and some were in wheelchairs. There was even a blind couple there. Michael looked like he'd opened a door to the chamber of horrors.'' Leroy's invigorating laughter overflowed pleasantly into my quiet living room. "He didn't lose any time in getting out of there, but what makes the whole thing so funny is that Michael always grumbles about the several disabled employees that Dad has at the bank. Every time he encounters one he says, 'When I take over this bank, I'm not going to be falling all over a bunch of cripples all the time!' The night of the meeting he really stepped into it, didn't he?''

I couldn't help laughing along with Leroy, and I could appreciate his humor about the matter, but deep inside me, Michael's unhealthy attitude about his brother, and perhaps other disabled persons, was beginning to sicken me. I wanted to question Leroy about how Michael had developed such insensitivity, but I thought maybe I shouldn't mention how much it troubled me. We had discussed it only once—on the first night he drove me home from work, when I had sensed that he might be trying to cover up Michael's behavior. He certainly didn't appear to be doing that now, but all I really knew about Michael's attitude was what he had said to me and what few remarks I had heard him make about Leroy at the candy shop. I decided to wait awhile before talking to Leroy any further about it, but I did want to clear up one remark he had just made.

"Michael won't really take over the bank someday, will he?''

Leroy peered at me over the edge of his goblet. "That's a lousy joke.''

I chuckled and said, "Tell me more about your HAL group.''

"Well, HAL is a consumer-advocacy organization trying to get a better life for disabled people. We try to help them by referring them to different agencies according to their needs, and we're constantly seeking opportunities for equal employment. We're a nonprofit organization, and both Dad and I serve on the board. We have members who are disabled and some who are not. Membership is five dollars a person; for students it's two dollars. Members receive a newsletter and are involved in the disabled movement. We have regular meetings to inform our members about different issues, and we also have parties, fellowships, and recreation.

"Anyone is welcome to join our organization whether he has a disability or not. A number of people have become interested in supporting our group. We have volunteers who help out on transportation committees and membership committees."

"Sounds like your group has thought of just about everything."

"Oh, there's more. We do sight checks for accessibility to different buildings, and the big thing we're working on now is special parking for the disabled at the different public places. After that we're going to tackle transportation. And we've also accepted the responsibility to make the public aware of the problems and the rights of disabled persons."

"Sounds like you've got your work cut out for you, but I don't doubt the group's success."

"A lot of the success, I think, has to do with the group's attitude. We're positive in our thinking. Some people have tried the hostile approach, but that isn't good and it hasn't accomplished anything.

"Businessmen are concerned with the costs of our proposed changes, and I think that's understandable. But a lot of what we're asking doesn't cost much—such as water fountains. They think they'll have to lower them, but all they need to do is add cups and a trash can. Of course, many changes are more complicated and costly than that. Mr. Reed has been one of the first to work with us. He installed an automatic open-and-close device on his door last year."

"Such a simple thing—maybe not inexpensive, but simple—

and it can be such a great help to a person with a handicap, or a disability, whichever you call it. I guess those two terms really amount to the same thing anyway.''

''Well, not really. We used Handicapped Action League for our group because the word 'handicapped' seemed to be more widely used among the general public. But 'handicapped' is a word correctly used to describe someone who has a physical or mental disability that interferes with that person leading a happy, productive life. So a person's disability may or may not be a handicap. It *becomes* a handicap if it interferes with his expectations for himself, his performance on the job, or his relationships with other people, such as his family and friends or society in general.''

''Then 'disability' is the right word to use in most situations?''

''Yes.''

''I guess a lot depends on a person's attitude toward a disabled person. I'm glad your group doesn't have to encounter many people like Michael.''

Leroy smiled gently. ''You must still be giving him a hard time. He wasn't in a very good mood when he came back from the candy shop one day last week.''

''If you call refusing to go out with him giving him a hard time, then I guess I did.''

''He asked you out and you said no?''

''Why do you keep reminding me of Bertha?'' I giggled like a schoolgirl. ''He asked me to go out to the lake and...well...you know.''

Leroy stared at his empty glass. ''I'm sorry. Michael doesn't—''

''It's all right. You don't have to apologize for him.''

''He should have sense enough to know a lady when he sees one.''

"Thank you."

Leroy kept staring at his glass. I stared at him.

"I don't understand why everyone's so bananas about your brother," I said at last. "Frankly, I like you much better."

He looked up at me. "You do?"

"Uh huh."

We gazed a little awkwardly at each other. "What did you do before you started to work at Mr. Reed's store?" he asked, breaking the silence.

"After I graduated from high school I traveled with my father for a year. He was an electronics engineer for a large firm here in town. Then I took a business course at a junior college. I took some creative writing courses too, and some courses in psychology. That's what I've been doing for the past year—going to college and writing a lot." Not wanting to leave Leroy wondering about my financial status and knowing he was too polite to inquire, I added, "When my father died he left me a trust fund. If I manage it wisely I should have enough money to last a long time. Sometimes I don't, though, but I think I'm learning more all the time about what it means to be a good steward, and not only of what I give to the Lord, but of what I keep for myself."

"Money means a lot to some people, but I found out a long time ago that it can't get you what's most important."

I watched Leroy for a long moment, wondering about the life he had had to live. I guessed that he had had to bear a lot of suffering, and not just physically but mentally as well.

"What's important to you?"

"People are important. Having respect for people and consideration for their feelings. And self-respect is important, and doing my best at what I can do."

"You can do just about anything you want to do, can't you?"

He nodded, chuckling softly. "I used to want to be a truck driver. Can't you just see that?"

"Why in the world would you want to be a truck driver?"

"The freedom, I guess. I've always wanted to ride around in one of those shiny chrome rigs and look out those big windows at the world going by. And I think being in command of all that power would really be something."

"If that's what you really want to do, you should do it."

He slapped his thighs. "With these legs?"

"You have special controls on your car, so why can't you get them on a truck, too?"

"There's a lot more to handling a big rig than driving a car; some of those things have 16 gears, and besides that, I couldn't climb in and out."

"What about a ramp or something to go up?"

"That'd be a lot of trouble to load and unload everywhere." He smiled his sunny smile. "A little boy who lives in the building where I've rented my apartment says he can hear me coming from the parking lot in my suit of armor. He calls me 'The Tin Soldier.' I think that's pretty funny."

I laughed along with Leroy.

"But tin soldiers don't drive trucks," he finished slowly.

I touched his arm. "Everybody has some kind of limitation in life—maybe it's not always physical, maybe it's mental or emotional—but there are always things we can't do."

"I understand what you're saying."

"I'll share something with you. I have a disability too, only it's not a disability, it's a real handicap. It's public speaking. I can't get up before groups of people and talk. It terrifies me. I become crippled and tongue-tied. My mind goes blank and my knees turn to jelly. Sometimes I actually get physically ill."

"That must be a terrible experience to go through."

"Nobody knows how dreadful it is. Even when I'm called on to pray at church, my heart pounds till I think it's going to explode. But I would never refuse to pray—in fact, I'm glad to do it. I don't know why I react so."

"That seems strange because one-on-one you're very outgoing."

"It puzzles me too, but I read somewhere that writers often have this problem, and the very fact that they can't speak publicly enables them to express themselves so well on paper. People who don't have problems with public speaking often can't say what they want to on paper. And then, of course, there are those talented few who can do both."

"I'll bet you could overcome the problem if you worked at it, if you really wanted to overcome it."

"I don't like to get up before people. I used to try because sometimes it's expected of me, like at church, but I don't even do that anymore because I go through so much."

"Your fear has become somewhat of a limitation."

"I know, but I'm who I am and I have to do what Holly English is capable of—with the Lord's help. And He can help me do all things. I know that even if I don't always apply it."

"I have a feeling that people are more disabled by what they *think* they can't do than by what they actually can't do."

"Something tells me you don't let your limitations keep you from the challenges of life. I'll bet if you really wanted to drive a truck you'd find a way. I'll bet you really like working at your father's bank."

"Yes, I do, and it pleases my mom and dad."

"But does it please you more?"

"Oh, yes. I enjoy meeting people, and figures fascinate me. There's almost no limit to what you can do with them. I probably should be an accountant, but I like what I'm doing. If

I can possibly make a loan for a person or a company, I will, but sometimes there just isn't any way to extend the desired amount of credit.''

"Not enough assurance of getting it back?"

"That's right, but credit expansion is the heart of banking. It allows banks and businesses and people to grow and progress. When a borrower draws against established credit, a bank adds this to its total deposits. This increases the bank's assets and helps other people, too.''

"It sounds interesting, but I don't have too much of a head for figures and detailed business.''

Leroy looked me steadily in the eye. "Why do you work if you don't have to? Writing and going to school must keep you busy.''

"I'm not going to school right now, and I wanted to go to work. I really like my job at Mr. Reed's. I like making sodas and sundaes, and meeting people, too. That's important to writing. People. Life and reactions to life gives the substance for stories. And then there's imagination to add to all that.''

"What kind of stories do you write?"

"I've written some short stories, but I haven't had any of them published. I send them off to magazines all the time, but they keep coming back. Sometimes I think I'd like to write a novel. It's a different form of writing from short stories, but I think I'd like it better. There's more character development, for one thing.''

"And you'd like that?"

"I guess I'm crazy, huh?"

"I don't know," he said and laughed deeply. It was beautiful.

"Do you like Chinese food?" I asked in a minute, and wondered why that question had popped into my head.

"Yes.''

"So do I, but I don't like to cook it."

"Cooking is a kind of hobby of mine."

"Really?"

He nodded. "I enjoy it a lot. I can cook Chinese food pretty well."

"I can eat it pretty well too!"

We grinned at each other, and then a kind of hesitant silence fell over the room.

"Writing is my hobby, I guess, but I'd sure like it to become more."

"It probably will in time."

"Yes, it does take time. That's mainly why I believe God wanted me to apply for the job at the candy shop. I know it's time I was contributing to my own upkeep, but mostly I'm contributing something and being a witness there till He's ready to use my writing—if that's what He wants me to do for Him. And I believe it is. Sometimes I feel like He's got something special planned for me to do, but it hasn't come along yet. So if I can just be patient and wait on Him, and if I can just keep my vanity under control...but it hurts so much to be rejected again and again when you've put all your heart and soul and effort into your work."

"I understand how you feel about trying and trying, but never quite making it. But vanity was one problem I never had. I was smothered with attention from well-meaning friends and relatives when I was growing up. And I appreciated how they felt. What I didn't like was the stares from strangers when I went out. Pity when it's given from kindness is one thing, but pity that's given because a person feels superior, or because someone doesn't know how to relate to me—that's something else. It's pretty hard to take. Disabled persons don't want to be looked down upon or pitied because circumstances beyond their control have made them a little different. We want to be accepted and treated as nearly as possbile the way anyone wants to be treated."

I thought about what Leroy said. "You know what's wrong with most people? They don't have enough empathy."

"Most of the people I come in contact with are used to me, and as for the others, I guess they can't help but stare. I know a big guy getting around on crutches is a sight, but I don't mind the looks anymore, now that I pretty well understand human nature."

"I think you get around very well."

Leroy glanced at his watch. "I guess I'd better be getting around to getting out of here."

I waited for him to move. He didn't. He sat very still, gazing at me, and I got the feeling that he was suddenly ill-at-ease and would have squirmed in his seat and shuffled his feet had he been able to.

Finally he stood up and reached for his crutches, propped against the wall nearby, then started across the floor. I got up and walked with him. A few feet from the door he came to a stop.

"I was wondering if I could ask you something."

"Sure."

He was gazing tenderly at me, and the soft light from my living room flickered warmly in his clear blue eyes. That funny little feeling shot over me again just then, but it came and went so fast that I didn't have time to figure out what it was.

Leroy smiled down on me and said, "I have two tickets for the Dinner Theatre Friday night, and I was wondering if you'd like to go with me...that is, if you don't have any other plans."

"I don't have any plans."

"Then you'll go?" he asked, his gentle eyes suddenly all glowing and bright.

"I'd like very much to go with you."

Chapter 7

It was the following night. I was doing my volunteer work. at the hospital. I didn't see Leroy at first. As usual I was absorbed in what Steve was saying. I watched the light dance in his eyes, blue-green and deep as the sea, I thought. The light danced in that deep blue-green and a glow came on in my heart. I studied his smile of perfect teeth and longed to run my fingers through his blond hair, almost the color of Leroy's, and blown casually back.

Steve was speaking more intensely now, and I watched his firm, full jawline as it moved in accordance with his words. I had to look way up at Steve—he was all of six feet tall, and his 170 pounds were distributed magnificently over a solid, expansive frame.

I glanced across the hospital lobby. Out of the corner of my eye I caught a glimpse of Leroy. He had pulled one of the wide entrance doors open and was trying to hold it out of his way with his back and shoulders. Watching him struggle with the heavy door made me realize just how important his work with HAL really was. I even felt a little ashamed at how easily I took for granted such simple tasks as opening doors—but not so simple when you're supported by crutches. But Leroy seemed to be taking the effort completely in his stride, for in a minute he put out his crutches and swung himself inside. He had been smiling when he entered the door, but when he saw me standing at the information desk talking to Steve his jaw fell.

Coming out from behind the long desk, I hurried over to greet him, calling his name as I went. "Leroy, hi!"

He smiled again. "Hi, Miss Good Luck!"

Steve walked up beside us then. "Leroy, I'd like you to meet a friend of mine."

After an exchange of introductions, an awkward silence fell over us. I looked up at the men on each side of me, both such fair and handsome young men and so similar in their friendly, easygoing personalities. Startled, I suddenly realized I was comparing them. I couldn't imagine why. It wasn't as though I had a choice between the two. Oh, I knew Leroy was growing to like me more and more—a woman can feel something like that—but Steve? Well, Steve liked me too. In fact, we were best of friends! I smiled, recalling that Steve and I had been friends since we first met here at the hospital, where he was taking his internship and I had come as a volunteer to help fill some of the lonely hours after my father's death. Steve and I gave each other understanding, truth, and companionship, and our friendship had flourished.

I had known Steve for a year-and-a-half. I had fallen in love with him the first time I saw him. It was difficult to explain how something like that happens. It just happens. You look at someone and your eyes meet and the next thing you know you feel kind of funny inside. From that moment on the world isn't the same anymore.

I thought about my dates with Steve—our "friendship" dates, he called them. We had done a lot of things together off and on. We went to movies and concerts and out to eat, and of course we went to church. Sometimes when Steve would take me home, he'd give my hand a warm squeeze or brush my cheek with a soft kiss, but there was never a time when I didn't long for more. Steve was a Greek name. It meant "crown." As far as I was concerned he deserved a crown. To me he was a prince, maybe even a king.

I was still looking up at my two attractive companions when Steve broke the uncomfortable silence.

"It sure is nice to meet a friend of Holly's" he said to Leroy. "Where did you two get together?"

Leroy went briefly over his acquaintanceship with me, mentioning his job at the bank and his love for Mr. Reed's hot fudge sundaes. Then, as he and Steve talked, Leroy suddenly caught my attention. Over his words, which were certainly friendly enough, he was studying Steve with such intensity that I thought his eyes would pop right out of his head. It struck me then that Leroy didn't know any of the circumstances surrounding my relationship with Steve. He probably thought he was someone I cared for very much. Well, he was right about that, but the circumstances weren't exactly as Leroy might be thinking they were. And I couldn't trust myself to ever explain them to him.

I was too afraid that my true feelings would show. I smiled discreetly, pleased that Leroy thought enough of me to be concerned about Steve.

While Leroy and Steve were getting acquainted, I surveyed the modern lobby of our new hospital, with its giant plants of fern and philodendron placed occasionally on the glossy floor and its silver-framed paintings of streams and forests hanging here and there on the natural walls. It was then that I heard it—the call over the intercom for Dr. Steve Gardner.

Leroy and Steve had deepened their conversation, Steve inquiring into Leroy's work at the bank, and Leroy obliging with quiet answers and then questions to Steve about his internship. Steve had graduated from medical school two years earlier, but he had been undecided about what field of medicine he wanted to enter. His recent work in the hospital's emergency room seemed to be leading him in the direction of surgery. I knew he was constantly seeking the Lord's will in the matter, and if God wanted him to become a surgeon I was certain he would be an outstanding one. Steve was so quick and steady, and his self-discipline was highly developed. I was proud of Steve and knew that I radiated a quiet glow standing there next to him.

"I think they're looking for you, doctor," I said.

He smiled his even smile. I called him "doctor" all the time of late, and it pleased him, I could tell.

"Hate to run off like this, Leroy," he said, "but duty calls."

Leroy offered his hand. "Nice meeting you, Steve."

"Same here. See you around." He winked at me and strode off in the direction of the emergency room.

I wished he hadn't winked. At least I wished Leroy hadn't seen it. It didn't mean anything special. It was just a part of Steve's friendly manner, but I was sure Leroy would draw a different conclusion. I ventured a glance in his direction.

He was wearing a frown and looking down at me.

I averted my gaze and stood there wishing I knew what to do next. Then, as if the Lord was intervening on my behalf before I even asked, the telephone rang and I went back around the desk to answer it.

Leroy followed me to the desk, and after I hung up he said, "I just came by to see if you needed a ride home. You were so nice last night to help me pick out those things for my apartment that I was wondering what I could do for you in return. Then I remembered you said you volunteered here on Tuesday nights." He glanced at his watch. "Visiting hours are almost over—do you get off then?"

"Yes. And thank you. It was very thoughtful of you to come by for me."

"I started once not to come. I thought you might have driven your car, but then I decided you probably came here right from work."

I nodded.

"Have you had dinner?"

"Yes. I always get a bite in the hospital cafeteria."

Leroy and I left the hospital parking lot and rode along talking now and then. Mostly I was thinking about Steve. He didn't affect me as much anymore. Of course, he didn't call or come by as much, but when I saw him at the hospital or church (he lived not far from there) he could still quietly turn my world upside down. When we weren't together, I was in almost complete control. I thought about him, naturally, but it was very different from the way things were in the beginning.

How excited I used to get just at the thought of seeing Steve! What better foundation for love to grow than a beautiful friendship, I thought. But Steve's feeling stopped at the bond of friendship while mine went soaring on to cozy little tete-a-tetes curled up in front of the fireplace in my apartment.

I stopped getting so excited at the prospect of seeing Steve shortly after he met Noreen. Before long I knew he was as much in love with her as I was with him.

Leroy pulled the car up to a red light at the intersection two blocks from the hospital. He looked over at me with a curious expression occupying his suntanned features. Our small bits of conversation had lapsed into total silence, and I knew he was wondering why. But what could I tell him? That's the way it was now. Instead of being left with giddy excitement after an encounter with Steve, and with happy anticipation of our next meeting, I struggled with quiet reflection and a reminder of the acceptance that had so slowly and painfully come to me following his first dates with Noreen. But the acceptance couldn't stop the feelings in my heart. I knew I still had a problem within myself. Maybe I would always have it.

"A penny for your thought," Leroy said as we pulled away from the red light.

I laughed self-consciously, knowing I had to somehow mask my feelings or they might suddenly pop conspicuously into view.

"I guess I was just sort of daydreaming."

"But it's night."

I smiled, appreciating Leroy's gentle humor.

"Anything I can help with?"

"Oh, no," I replied hastily. Aware that I could offer no explanation for my strange behavior, I sought to change the subject.

Talking casually with Leroy, I gazed over thoughtfully at him. He really was a sweet man—so gentle and understanding . God couldn't have given me a better companion to share my life. I sent a quick, silent prayer of thanks toward heaven and suddenly wondered if Leroy knew God, really knew Him in a per-

sonal way. He had mentioned the Bible that first evening he
had taken me home, and he didn't seem surprised or put off
whenever I spoke of my Christian life. I like Leroy. I knew we
were going to be dear friends, and it was so important to me
to know if he was a Christian. I decided that we knew each other
well enough for me to ask him such a personal question.

But when I turned to speak to Leroy it seemed he could almost
read my mind, for he said, "Holly, where do you go to church?"

For a minute I was taken aback and sat thinking about the
place of my worship. Steve had told me about it shortly after
I began volunteering at the hospital. When I discovered that
the church Steve attended was not far from my new apartment,
even close enough to walk to, I was delighted and soon made
it my own, as Steve had done. How wonderful it was to be able
to go anywhere in this country and find a family, the loving
family of God, where I truly belonged!

"I go to a small church just a few blocks from where I live.
It's close to your place, too. It's such a warm church and so
filled with the Spirit. We try to live close to the Scriptures, and
we're very mission-minded."

"Now that I've got my own apartment, I've been wondering
about a church around here somewhere."

What Leroy said pleased me. It meant that he was interested
in church, but I knew that it didn't necessarily mean he was
a Christian.

"I'd be very happy if you'd give our church a try. I'm sure
you'll like it."

He smiled over at me. "I'm sure I will, too."

I gazed reflectively at Leroy for a minute. This seemed to
be a good time to ask him, so I just blurted it out. "Leroy,
have you accepted Jesus as your Savior?"

"No, Holly, I don't think I have. I've gone to church all my life, but I've had some problems with that ever since I was stricken with polio. Oh, I've never really *blamed* God, but when it happened I was 11, and I reasoned that it was contrary to everything I'd been taught. From the time I was old enough to understand what words meant, I'd been told that Jesus loved me. But I couldn't fit that in with the pain and struggling I had to go through and the paralysis I was left with for the rest of my life. I don't think I've ever fit it in. I grew up not quite understanding this God of ours. I had a lot of questions but I never found any answers.

"When I was 13 I made a profession of faith, but I don't think it was real to me. I just did it because everyone else did. It was expected of me.

"I remember everyone was so glad that day, especially my mom and dad, but inside I didn't feel glad. I didn't feel anything. Going down the aisle that Sunday morning was just part of church—everybody did it sooner or later."

My heart grew heavy at Leroy's words. "But surely you know what it really means to step out and give your life to Jesus?"

By this time we had arrived at my apartment and Leroy had pulled up before the walkway and turned off the engine. "I know what it means to some people," he said, gazing levelly at me. "It means everything to you, I can tell." He looked away suddenly. "I think I'd like it to be real to me the way it is to you."

"Oh, it can be!"

He turned. "How?"

"By really taking hold of Him through faith," I said, rejoicing at his willingness to try. "And He'll give you the grace to really believe."

"What happens to my questions?"

"Maybe He won't give you all the answers here and now.

Life holds so many mysteries. You may have to wait till you're on the other side for all the answers. But just to know you belong to Him is what really counts.''

Leroy looked at me with new light in his eyes. "Now we see through a glass darkly, but then face to face; now I know in part, but then I shall know even as also I am known."

"First Corinthians 13:12," I echoed, smiling, and then I laid my hand on his arm. "Yes."

"I've searched the Scriptures for the answers to my questions, but I can't seem to find them."

I was touched by his sincerity. "Maybe you will. Don't give up."

He took my hand in his and gave it a tender squeeze. Then we got out of the car and walked to my door, and Leroy came in without any coaxing. He took a place on the couch, and I saw Chow Mein jump up beside him as I went into the kitchen to make some coffee.

"Do you take anything in your coffee?" I called.

"No, I drink it black."

I came back shortly with two cups and set them on the coffee table. Chow Mein left for the bowl of milk I'd set out for him in the kitchen.

"I hope you don't mind instant," I said, sitting down next to Leroy.

"That's fine."

I watched him lean over and lift one of the cups to his mouth. When he had replaced the cup in its saucer, I said, "No one could blame you if you felt some bitterness about your disability."

"Why should I be bitter?"

I glanced down at his still legs, confined beneath his trousers in those long braces of leather and steel. "I'm glad you're not, but I think you have at least two good reasons."

"Because my legs are paralyzed? That's no reason. Like I said, there's some things I don't understand, but I can't help what happened to me. I'd rather be like I am than be like Michael is."

I thought about what Leroy said and considered it a terrible choice to have to make—something like the lesser of two evils.

"You said you were 11 when you got polio. That must have been right before the oral vaccine was discovered."

He nodded.

"I guess you've spent a lot of time wondering why they couldn't have discovered it a little sooner."

"I'm just glad no more kids have to go through what I've been through. It was pretty hairy, the therapy and all."

"Polio is caused by a virus, isn't it?"

"The viruses attack the brain and spinal cord. They enter the body through the mouth and nose and go to the central nervous system and enter a nerve cell and make it work for them instead of the body. Paralysis results when many nerve cells are destroyed."

"It sounds horrible."

"I had spinal paralytic polio. It's the most common form. The viruses attack the nerve cells that control the muscles of the limbs and trunk."

"If I tried I don't think I could even begin to imagine it."

"Don't try—you don't want to know."

I tried to smile sympathetically, but deep inside I knew I could never fully understand why God allowed such things as disease and crippling, and for that matter, things like blindness and deafness—all the disabilities. Yet I wanted so much to help Leroy overcome the feelings that might be keeping him from making a personal commitment to God. Whatever the reasons for some of the things we had to bear in life, we didn't have to go through them alone. Jesus promised us life more abundant, and I knew He didn't mean that the abundant life was all to come later in heaven.

"Maybe God has allowed you to suffer this disability because of your attitude. You set such a good example for other people. Most people need someone to look up to." I grinned. "A sort of knight in shining armor."

Leroy's smile was bigger than mine. "I don't know about that, but I *have* tried to accept what happened and what I am because of it, and go on from there."

"That's great. Even though I'm a Christian, if it were me I'd probably hate something or someone, at least a little bit."

"No, you wouldn't, not you. And besides, hate can weigh you down." He rested his hands on his thighs. "Having to carry all this armor around is bad enough without adding that."

Leroy took a drink of his coffee, and I couldn't help but stare at him in admiration. His disability meant less to me than it ever had, if indeed it had ever meant anything to me at all. I was sorry Leroy's legs were paralyzed; I was sorry he had to wear heavy braces on them; and I wished I could have been there in days gone by; I wished I could have borne some of the pain and struggling for him. And for an instant I wished for the power to wipe it all away and give him a perfect body—but I knew I couldn't and I didn't feel any pity for him. Some people needed pity. Leroy didn't.

Later that night, after Leroy had gone, I lingered a long time over my private devotions with God. I prayed with all my heart that Leroy would genuinely respond to the Holy Spirit's call.

Chapter 8

I was busy in Mr. Reed's office all the next morning. There was filing to be done and letters to be typed and even some figures to be balanced in the bookkeeping ledger. Now and then I hummed a little tune along with the hum of the heater on the tropical-fish tank which sat just inside the door. Once I glanced up at the sign hanging on the wall above the desk. I paused to read it for what seemed like the hundredth time:

Life Is An Echo

What you send out—comes back. What you sow—
you reap. What you give—you get. What you see

in others—exists in you. Regardless of who you are
or what you do, if you are looking for the best way
to reap the most reward in all areas of life, you
should look for the best in every person and in
every situation and adopt The Golden Rule as a
way of life.

I smiled as I thought about the fine Christian gentleman who
had hung the sign there. I knew he was fast becoming a kind
of combination father/grandfather figure to me. He was relaxed
and sympathetic, and I could talk to him about almost anything.
It was a joyful time in my life when I came to work for him.
I smiled again and remembered the day of my job interview
with my employer. It was a beautiful morning in April, crisp
and sunny. I had read Mr. Reed's ad in the paper the previous
night and I had prayed for God's guidance before I went to
sleep. Mr. Reed's smile had been as sunny as the day, and I
knew before the interview was half over that he wanted to hire
me as much as God wanted me to accept.

When I went out to the front of the store that afternoon
following lunch, Michael was the first customer to come in.
What kind of Christian did I seem to him, I pondered? I didn't
ponder long.

If I hadn't known better, I would have thought that someone
else was disguised in Michael's body that day. He was so quiet!
He didn't joke with Bertha and he hardly spoke to me. He just
ordered a pineapple malt and paid in silence. I was about to
credit his mood to a bad day at the office, but just as he was
going out the door Cara returned from her lunch break with
several packages loaded in her arms. Michael swept grandly onto
the sidewalk, colliding with Cara and her packages. I don't know
what I expected him to do—maybe admonish her for not get-

ting out of the way of Michael Britton—but whatever I expected I didn't think he would ever do what he did.

At once his arm shot out to steady Cara on her feet, and then he bent to retrieve her packages and stack them one by one in her outstretched arms, words of apology pouring from his lips in a low, steady stream. I got the sudden feeling that I was watching Leroy instead of Michael, except for the obvious difference in their abilities.

How completely out of character, I mused as Cara made her way numbly into the shop and Michael took off with male nonchalance up the sidewalk. Reviewing the incident and Michael's entire visit set me to wondering if there was a side to him that none of us knew. I had detected a small amount of hidden charm in him once before. Could it be that a drop or two of decent humility actually existed somewhere beneath that flamboyant exterior? It was to be some time before I would get the answer to my question, for later in the day, at closing time, Michael came back to the shop with Linda Benton. He was easily recognizable this time. He bought Linda a Coke and laughed and joked and in general carried on as usual. He even managed to squeeze in a crack about Leroy and why he wasn't at the shop, since it was almost time for me to get off.

"He rushed right out of his office a little before five and headed straight for his car. He must have big plans for tonight." He winked at me but I ignored him.

I crossed the street and directed my steps toward the bus stop. I couldn't help but wonder about Leroy as I walked along. Since the first night he had taken me home, he had appeared at the shop nearly every night with the same offer. It was becoming a routine, and I wondered what could be important enough to take him somewhere directly after work. Perhaps something had come up with HAL.

I was lost in thought when I happened to notice Cara coming across the street at a leisurely pace. The plainness of her features struck me—her dull, straight hair and her acne-covered cheeks. Watching her move slowly in my direction, I thought back to how Leroy had greeted her in the candy shop the first day I had met him—"Hi, Hardwork."

Hardwork. That was an apt description of Cara. She came to work every morning promptly at eight, did her job, and left exactly at five (unless Mr. Reed needed her to get out a last-minute candy order). Nothing much happened in between. Cara was nice to the customers, responding when they initiated conversation, but she didn't strike out on her own with anyone—seldom even with Leroy, and she really seemed to like him. Cara was another puzzle to me. I wondered about her life away from the candy shop, and I wondered if she were a Christian. My natural curiosity pushed me to find out.

When she stepped up from the curb, I approached her with a sudden idea.

"Are you in a hurry to get home tonight, Cara?"

She shrugged and shook her head.

"Well, I was thinking. You didn't look hurried and I'm not either." I thought ahead to prayer meeting at 7:30, but this was more important. I might even skip prayer meeting if things worked out. I knew Steve would be there, and seeing him was always a pleasure, but Cara was my concern of the moment. I would do what I knew God wanted me to do and let the other things take care of themselves.

"I was thinking maybe you and I could go somewhere for a bite to eat. We've been working together for awhile now, but we really haven't had much of a chance to get acquainted."

Cara seemed taken by surprise at my idea, and at first I

thought she was going to say no. "It's nice of you to ask me, Holly."

It occurred to me then that I really didn't know a thing about Cara. She appeared to be anything but prosperous. Perhaps she couldn't afford to eat out. I considered whether I should offer to treat or not, but decided that it might offend her.

I was about to blurt out who knows what kind of suggestion when she said, "Where would you like to go?"

We went back across the street, down the block and around the corner, past the bank, to the restaurant where Leroy and I had gone the night we picked out the furnishings for his apartment. I learned much about Cara that evening. With just the two of us in a booth at the quiet restaurant, she was more talkative than she was at the candy shop. She told me that she lived at home with her parents, both of whom had recurring drinking problems. She had four younger brothers and sisters at home (she was my age), and two of them were twins. It was purchases for the twins that she had been carrying that afternoon when she and Michael had collided. They were having a birthday on Saturday, and Cara was keeping their gifts at the shop till then.

As Cara and I chatted, I noticed a look in her hazel eyes that I hadn't seen before. It was deep and wise, and I sensed that she was a young woman more mature than her years. I credited this to her home life, for some of the things she said revealed that most of the responsibility of caring for her brothers and sisters fell on her shoulders.

I soon found I was feeling sorry for my new friend. She didn't seem to have much life after her job and her responsibilities at home. As our conversation neared an end, I was caught up in telling Cara about our singles class at church and how much fun we had doing things together. I told her about recent activities—a skating party and spring banquet. But what seemed to interest Cara most was what I told her about why our group came together in the first place.

"It's a common bond that draws us, the greatest kind of bond—our love for Jesus Christ and our desire to live like His brothers and sisters."

"Could I be a part of that bond?" Cara asked with a painful, lonely kind of sound in her voice.

"Oh, yes!"

"Could I join your group?"

"Nothing would please us more than to have you in our group. Why don't you come to church this Sunday? That would be a good time for you to get acquainted with everyone."

"I'd really like to but I don't know. I probably don't have anything proper to wear."

"Wear anything you like—a dress, pants, whatever. You'll be right at home. Our church is small and comfortable. You needn't worry about clothes."

Cara smiled a sweet little smile. "Maybe I *will* come, Holly, maybe I will."

"I'm counting on it. We could really use a level-headed girl like you to help us out. Sunday we'll be discussing one of our mission projects, a plan to help send inner-city kids to a Christian camp later this summer."

"Oh, but I'm not a Christian."

So I had the answer to my question. "Would you like to be a Christian, Cara?"

"I think I would, yes. If being a Christian means being like you. Oh, I know I'm not as pretty as you, but you have something that shines from inside. If being a Christian is how you got that, then I'd like to be a Christian too."

Cara was truly seeking, I could tell. In my heart I prayed

silently as I explained God's plan of salvation. It was a beautiful sight when right there in the booth at the restaurant, with soft lights pouring over us and quiet music flowing about us, Cara bowed her head and accepted Jesus as her Savior and asked Him to forgive her sins and come into her heart. I looked up once and caught sight of several people gaping strangely at us as they passed, but I just smiled and didn't even try to hide the tears of joy spilling unrestrained down my cheeks.

Walking back to the bus stop, I was too excited to take much notice of anything, so I didn't hear everything that Cara was saying. I know I answered a few questions she had about being a Christian. My answers seemed to come automatically from many years of being in church. Then suddenly one question Cara tossed at me brought me abruptly back to reality. It wasn't so much the question I'd heard, but the mention of Leroy's name.

"What did you say?"

"I said, are you falling in love with Leroy?"

I must have looked quite astonished because then Cara reddened slightly and said, "Oh, I'm sorry. I know it's really none of my business."

"It's all right. Your question just took me by surprise, that's all."

"Well, are you? Are you in love with Leroy?"

We had arrived at the bus stop by this time and I halted my steps not far from the curb of the deserted street. The sun had slipped behind the nearby tall buildings, and they loomed dark and mysterious against the blaze of an orange-pink sky. I stared at Cara, wondering why I hadn't answered her. I summoned my voice, but it seemed to be off somewhere on a mission of its own. I cleared my throat, or tried to, but no sound came. Suddenly I wondered how Cara felt about Leroy. I knew she liked him, but maybe her feelings went deeper than that. It occurred to me then what a bewilderment I was to myself sometimes. Why should I care how Cara felt about Leroy? Why should I care how any girl felt about him? We were just friends. Nothing more.

I told Cara as much. She gazed at me with a funny little grin on her plain, blemished face.

"I'm not in love with Leroy," I said finally, glad that my voice had decided to stay with me. "What makes you ask?"

"Oh, I don't know. Maybe it's the way you smile when he comes in the shop and the way you look at him sometimes. You kind of glow from inside—that shine, y'know?"

Cara's words shocked me, and for a minute I was afraid I'd lose my voice again, although I certainly didn't know why, so I spoke quickly. "How do you feel about him?"

"I don't think I've ever met anybody as nice as he is, and I think it's just awful that he's crippled. It's not fair."

"I couldn't agree with you more, but I guess there's nothing for us to do but accept it like Leroy has and not let it bother us any more than he lets it bother him." I looked up to see my bus coming along the street. "Well, I've got to go now." I put my arm about Cara and gave her a kiss on the cheek. "Good night—I'll see you in the morning."

Cara's sweet smile lingered in my memory as I boarded the bus and took a seat near the door. I glanced at my watch. It was only 6:30! So much had taken place in such a short time! I was beginning to get excited again. I had just enough time to get home and feed Chow Mein before hurrying over to prayer meeting. I couldn't wait to share with Steve the good news of Cara's conversion at the restaurant.

Chapter 9

⋘⋙

When I arrived at church, Steve and Noreen were already seated. I sat down in the pew beside them. We often sat together, the three of us, and other members of our Bible study class. We were all such good friends. No one knew about the deep love in my heart for Steve, or about the even deeper hurt. I didn't want anyone to ever know, especially Steve. I was afraid that it might spoil our close friendship, and, besides, I thought very highly of Noreen and wouldn't have done anything that might have caused her even the slightest concern.

Noreen was so right for Steve. The daughter of a seminary

professor, she was well-schooled in her faith, and her serious but warm personality so complimented his own. I was sorry I couldn't have been the girl of Steve's choosing. I had wanted that more than anything in the world, but if it couldn't be me, I couldn't have chosen a more perfect girl for him than Noreen.

I arrived at church sooner than I had expected and had finished sharing my good news about Cara when Noreen got up and excused herself to check on some Bible study materials. Steve and I remained, talking about his job and mine, when unexpectedly I sensed Leroy's presence in the church. I wasn't aware of how I knew he was there, yet momentarily I turned, expecting to see him in the aisle. But he wasn't there. The aisle was empty. Everyone had taken a seat, since the service was only minutes from beginning.

Noreen returned and I sat perplexed, staring at the door. Finally I jumped up and hurried down the aisle. The foyer was deserted except for a small child. I don't know what made me walk over to the door and go out on the porch—just that "sixth sense," that intuitive power that makes a person act in spite of the seemingly obvious. But when I did go outside I saw Leroy descending the last of the many steps and starting along the walk to the parking lot. I sped down the steps after him.

He stopped and turned as I approached, appearing both glad and surprised to see me. But when I smiled and spoke, he only looked down at the sidewalk, standing there as though he was planted solidly in the concrete. I could tell he was extremely embarrassed about something, and I didn't know what to say. If I had looked forward to Leroy visiting our church, I certainly hadn't expected him until Sunday. That was when most people visited. But he had chosen to come tonight (so that was why he had hurried from work), and I was genuinely confused about why he was leaving.

In my usual outspoken manner I finally asked him. This only embarrassed him further—he was already crimson-faced and close-mouthed—and I thought he was going to turn and walk away.

I touched his arm, feeling such a tenderness toward him all of a sudden. "Don't go—let's go back inside."

"I shouldn't have come. I guess I assumed you'd be by yourself. When I saw you with your friend Steve, I started to take a seat in the back, since I came for the service, but then I felt foolish for coming at all without letting you know, and I thought it would be better to leave."

"But why should you do that? You should've come and sat with us."

"Oh, no. You're with someone else."

"I'm not with anyone else. I was just sitting with Steve and his girlfriend. She had gone to get something and she was coming right back. But of course you couldn't know...about Noreen, I mean."

Leroy's disheartened expression changed completely. He even managed one of his beautiful smiles.

"Come on, we'd better get back inside," I said. "The service has probably already started."

"How did you know I was here?" he asked as we mounted the steps. "You couldn't have seen me, since you were talking to Steve."

It came to me then how I had been aware of Leroy's presence. "I heard you coming," I grinned, "like a knight in shining armor."

Leroy slipped into another smile, then he started to laugh. I looked over at him, studying his face above mine. He was so handsome and his smile really was like sunshine—so bright and warm.

Going up the many steps was slow work for Leroy. Noticing his effort, I was acutely reminded of another of the many blessings I took for granted every day. Climbing steps seemed so easy, just like opening doors.

"Going up all these steps really reinforces my belief in HAL," Leroy said.

I understood exactly what he meant. Climbing the steps with braces on his legs wasn't easy, but he made steady progress and at last we reached the wide front porch.

"Having a ramp up to this porch would be great, wouldn't it?"

Leroy beamed. "It would be wonderful! Then it wouldn't take me half the worship hour to get to the door."

We laughed quietly and went inside.

After the service I introduced Leroy to almost everyone who came our way, and he was cheerfully invited to come back for Sunday worship. We were about to get up and leave when Steve and Noreen approached our pew. Steve greeted Leroy and introduced him to Noreen; then, while Leroy was taking up his crutches, Steve casually reached down and picked up my purse and Bible and gave them to me. I had some other books, too, ones that I had checked out of the church library.

"Would you like me to carry those?" Steve asked.

It was a natural gesture on his part, one that he made many times, and I didn't think anything about it. I thanked him and our eyes met and held in deep mutual affection. A minute later, when I happened to look over at Leroy, he was staring at us with an expression on his face that I couldn't quite describe. It seemed to be a mingle of hurt and grief with a measure of anger thrown in.

When Leroy realized I was looking at him, he dropped his gaze and turned and made his way down the aisle. I puzzled briefly over the incident, but when I joined him outside and pleasant conversation flowed I soon forgot the awful expression he had worn.

Leroy took me home later, but he didn't come inside when he walked me to the door. He said he was tired and wanted to get home because tomorrow would be a long, busy day with meetings at the bank and a meeting after work with HAL.

That night before going to sleep, I said another special prayer for Leroy's conversion, and I prayed for Cara and her new Christian walk.

On Sunday morning both Cara and Leroy came to church, and first there was Bible study class and discussion of our inner-city mission project for the children. When a definite plan of action had been decided upon, we adjourned for the worship hour. I sat beside Leroy at the back of the sanctuary, praying in my heart for his conversion, but when the invitation came and only Cara went forward from our pew to share the change in her life and make her acceptance of Christ a public confession of faith, I decided I was trying to rush things. This was a decision that only Leroy could make, and it would have to come in his own time, when he had settled the questions in his heart and mind. The concern I had then was that Leroy had spent 16 years of his life trying to settle the questions and yet he seemed no closer to the answers than he did when he began. Right then, as we were leaving at the close of the service, I asked God to use me in some specific way to help Leroy become a Christian.

Leroy offered Cara a ride home, but she declined rather timidly, saying something about stopping at the market near her house to pick up some food for lunch for her brothers and sisters, and that she'd better hurry to catch her bus.

As I watched Cara walk down the street to the bus stop at

the next corner, I thought about what a sweet person she had turned out to be, and I wondered if she ever dated. It seemed doubtful. She must be lonesome for some nice young man's company, I mused. I glanced at Leroy, for I guess I believed she liked him more than she admitted. Michael had even said one time that Cara was Leroy's type. Of course, he had meant to be insulting, and I couldn't rely on a statement like that. Suddenly a wild thought struck me. With the makeup and hairdo tricks I knew (thanks to a model friend), Cara could be made much more attractive. A proper cleansing and diet program were in order for her complexion, and there were several effective ways to cover the blemishes on her cheeks and many becoming ways to arrange her plain hair. Then maybe some nice young man would take more notice of her. I looked at Leroy again. Well, what will be will be, and who was I to stand in the way of love!

After Cara disappeared from sight into the long blue-and-white bus, I vowed to have a talk with her about making herself more attractive. I only hoped I could do it without being too blunt and maybe offending her. Cara had a nice, trim figure and her clothes were clean and pressed. Most of all, she had a pleasing personality once you broke the ice, so why should she spend all her time working and caring for her brothers and sisters? She was entitled to more of life than that, and now that she was a Christian I knew that God would help her have it.

Just then Steve and Noreen approached and asked Leroy and me to join them for lunch and a movie that afternoon. My heart froze! I looked at Leroy with I don't know what kind of expression on my face. We could all be friends, even attend the same class at church, but double-date with Steve—how could I bear it? I was near panic when I heard Leroy graciously decline their invitation.

"I had a sort of surprise planned for Holly this afternoon." He glanced at me and there was such a tender look in his eyes that I was deeply touched. I knew he really did have something wonderful planned for us that day.

We said good-bye to Steve and Noreen and were in Leroy's car driving down the street before I spoke. "You didn't say anything about special plans for today."

"Well...what I have in mind is special to me...but anyway, you didn't look like you wanted to go when Steve made his suggestion."

"It wasn't that I didn't want to go," I said quickly. Oh, I wanted to go all right, I thought—with Steve. I stole a sideways glance at Leroy, knowing that what I'd offered wasn't a very good explanation. I wanted to say more but knew I couldn't without betraying my true feelings, so I cast about in my mind for some way to change the subject. Leroy came to my rescue.

"I was going out to the lake later this afternoon to take my boat out. The wind should be good out there by then." He glanced briefly at me. "If you aren't doing anything, would you like to go with me?"

I smiled and nodded eagerly.

"What kind of plans do you have for lunch?"

"I'll probably go home and make something for Chow Mein and me—any old thing. I'm not very good in the kitchen."

"You cook for your cat?"

There was Leroy sounding like Bertha again. It wasn't so much the questions he asked but the way he asked—so doubtful and almost defiant, just like Bertha.

"Well, why not? He's all I have."

Leroy threw his head back and laughed. It filled the car with a deep, soft sound. "You just don't strike me as the cook-for-your-cat type."

"'Cooking for him usually consists of opening a can and warming the contents. That's what I do for myself, too. I'm afraid I'm not very domesticated."

"Why don't we go over to my apartment and I'll fix lunch. I'd like you to see how everything looks that we bought the other night, too."

I smiled my agreement. "I don't believe you really like to cook."

"Why not? I'm not half-bad."

No, you're not bad at all, I thought. In fact, you're pretty good, a good friend to have. Suddenly I thought of what Bertha had said about Leroy when she and I were talking in the lounge at the candy shop about a week earlier: "Poor ol' Leroy—he's everybody's friend but nobody's date." Well, he had been my date and we were planning to go out next Saturday to hear the Imperials Quartet, and what about today—wasn't this sort of a date?

It occurred to me then that I was beginning to see a lot of Leroy, and although I would have rather been with Steve, being with Leroy was nice. Yes, very nice. And it seemed that I didn't think about Steve as much when I was with Leroy.

"You don't strike me as the cook-for-yourself type," I said, picking up the conversation.

He grinned playfully at me. "Oh? Well, what type do I strike you as?"

"Let me see," I replied, gazing at the side of his smooth, handsome face. "I bet you're the type who likes to read."

"Yes, I do. I read a lot."

"And I bet you like good music."

He nodded, smiling.

"And I bet you like boats."

"Sailboats."

"You're so much fun," I said, laughing again. "And I feel honored that you want to cook for me."

We had pulled up to Leroy's apartment by this time. He turned off the ignition and looked over at me with the sweetest expression on his face. "I really like you, Holly," he said in his flowing voice. "I like you...more than I've ever liked any girl."

Suddenly Leroy did something very tender and beautiful. He reached for my hands and took them in both of his. His touch was powerful, yet so gentle and controlled. He held my hands for a minute, then drew them to his lips and placed a soft kiss on my fingers. I was almost overcome by his unexpected display of feeling, and as we got out of the car I was keenly aware that I had no idea of the degree of sensitivity that stirred deep within the heart of this kind, gentle young man with the crippled legs.

Chapter 10

I was a little nervous as we drove up the long, winding drive that led to the home of Leroy's parents. We had stopped at my apartment, where I had changed into jeans, T-shirt, and canvas shoes. I had twisted my long black hair into braids and Leroy had given me a white sailor hat. It was too big, of course, but I thought it looked rather cute. I glanced down at my casual attire and wondered what Mr. and Mrs. Britton would think.

When I mentioned this to Leroy, he laughed and put me off by saying, "You'd sure look silly going sailing in a frilly dress. Mom and Dad would think I'd brought along a real nut."

Mr. and Mrs. Britton lived in a magnificent, rambling brick house settled among tall, stately oaks and pines, and overlooking one end of enormous Lake Wyeth.

It was a joy meeting Leroy's father, a distinguished-looking and surprisingly relaxed man; and his mother, a serenely beautiful and gently bred woman. But upon arrival we didn't spend too much time at the house visiting with his parents, for Leroy was too anxious to get down to the lake and his beloved boat, a sloop he had named "The Maria Elena." He said he named it after the song. He thought it was the most beautiful song he had ever heard.

It was a lovely afternoon, just right for sailing, Leroy said, with a lazy sun playing flirtatiously on the vivid blue water and a warm, energetic wind stirring boldly beneath a pale, cloud-softened sky. As soon as we got aboard Leroy's 25-foot boat he proudly began explaining some of the exciting sport of sailing and how he loved the pleasure of leisurely hours on the water as well as the challenge that sailing brought to his skill as a sailor. Having an insatiable curiosity and positively no experience with sailboats, I was totally absorbed in his every word. When we got through the basics—his showing me the parts of the boat and the function of each—we went quickly onto the art of sailing itself and the three basic maneuvers.

"A boat sails because a sail has curved edges so it will be shaped like the wing of an airplanne when the wind fills it out," Leroy began. "The side of the sail to leeward, away from the wind, corresponds to the top of an airplane wing. The action of the wind blowing across this curved surface creates a lift similar to the force that enables an airplane to stay in the air. In a sailboat, this lifting force becomes a pull away from the sail and toward the bow of the boat. At the same time, the wind also exerts a push against the other side of the sail. In this way, the action of the wind on the sail combines in two ways to force the boat forward. This makes it possible to sail a boat in almost any direction.''

"Can you sail directly into the wind?''

"No boat can sail *directly* into the wind. If it does, the sail flaps like a flag and becomes useless. But a boat can sail upwind by tacking—that is, following a zigzag course. Generally a sailboat can head to within 45 degrees of the direction from which the wind is blowing before its sail starts to luff, or flap, and lose its driving force.

"We call sailing into the wind 'tacking to windward' or 'sailing on the wind,' '' Leroy continued. "This requires tremendous skill because the wind almost never blows constantly with the same force from the same direction. The speed that a sailor tacks brings him to a certain point upwind depending on his ability to feel the little shifts and changes in the wind, and to trim his sails accordingly.

"We call sailing across the wind 'reaching.' Boats can usually move faster when sailing across the wind than in any other direction.

"Sailing with the wind is called 'sailing before the wind' or 'running.' Running is not as fast as reaching. In running, the sail is simply pushed along by the wind and makes it's own resistance.

"Now let me explain about trimming and tacking—if you're with me so far.''

I let out a long sigh. I had an eager curiosity but a limited comprehension; nevertheless, I smiled and tried not to look too stupid and confused.

I don't think I succeeded, however, because then Leroy said, "I'll explain each maneuver again as we go into them further out on the water.''

I learned that trimming the sails meant adjusting them to obtain the full advantage of the available wind, and that a sailor must always know the wind direction in order to trim the sails correctly. Leroy said that when a boat is running before the wind, the mainsail should be at right angles to the boat's direction, and when a boat sails across wind, the mainsail must extend about halfway out from the boat, or at about a 45-degree angle to its direction of travel. When a boat sails into the wind, the sails must be trimmed as parallel as possible to the boat's direction.

Leroy cautioned that small sailboats can easily capsize if mishandled. He said that experienced sailors know where to place their weight and how to relieve dangerous pressure on the sails if a boat tips too far. This is done by "slacking off," he explained: letting the sails out so some of the wind spills from them.

Tacking, Leroy told me, involved turning the boat so that the wind comes at you from the opposite side when sailing into the wind. This is called "coming about." In coming about, the bow is turned so that the wind crosses it. This was a comparatively safe maneuver, Leroy said, but when the stern is to the wind, a turn called "jibbing," that brings the wind to the other side of the boat, causing the wind to cross the stern quickly and slamming the sail across the boat. This quick shift of forces, Leroy pointed out, could capsize a boat if the maneuver were not handled carefully and with skill.

Following a long afternoon of enjoying Leroy's splendid ability on the water, we tied up at the dock and were departing for shore when I slipped unexpectedly and unbecomingly on the wet deck. I don't know how Leroy did it, but he quickly discarded one crutch and reached for me, and, instead of falling on my embarrassment, I found myself caught securely in his right arm. His power was immense! So was our laughter!

At the house, Mr. and Mrs. Britton were waiting on the patio for us with some refreshment. It was a delightful evening, getting acquainted with Leroy's family and watching the moon rise above the black forest and cast silver shadows on the dark waters of the lake. From our conversation I surmised that I was one of the few girls that Leroy had brought home to meet his parents, and one of an exclusive minority that he had invited on his boat. Watching him talking animatedly with his mother and father, I was suddenly consumed with infinite pride at being the young woman he chose to favor with his time and pleasures. The tenderness I had felt toward him once before touched my heart in a new way. The feeling stayed with me as we drove back to my apartment.

Leroy came in with me; I made coffee and we sat on the couch talking casually. Leroy sipped the coffee from a stoneware mug. Once Chow Mein came by and solicited his usual amount of strokes from my obliging companion, then left us for his bowl of milk in the kitchen.

"I really liked having you on 'The Maria Elena' with me today," Leroy said in his smooth voice. "It felt good to share it with you."

"I had a good time out on the water and then talking with your parents. They seem so nice."

"They liked you, I could tell."

"Your mother is lovely. You look a lot like her."

"Thank you. That's a compliment to me. She was my best friend during a lot of rough times. When I got polio, she really took it all like a trouper. She was great. And afterward she tried to make up for all the things I couldn't do anymore, like climbing trees and playing ball, but she saw that there were other things. I could never tell her that nothing or no one could make up for those things, because she really tried."

"I've heard mothers are like that."

"I wish you could've known someone like my mother when you were growing up."

"Me too, but...well, you had your problems and I had mine. Now they're all behind us." I glanced at Leroy's crutches propped obtrusively against the wall nearby.

"My dad was great about everything too," Leroy went on. "Both my parents were. They accepted me and what happened to me, and that helped me accept myself. They never stopped letting me know they approved of me as a person. They didn't always approve of everything I did, and they let me know that too, but they always believed in me."

"I've often thought about what a job my father had when I was growing up. He had to be both mother and father to me, and I know it wasn't easy. But he was a strong believer in the Scriptures, and he taught me that as long as you go by what's written there you can survive any kind of circumstances."

"He sounds like a wise man."

"His favorite verse of Scripture was Philippians 4:13."

"I can do all things through Christ, who strengthens me."

I looked at Leroy in surprise. Sometimes he surely didn't act like a man who *hadn't* received Christ.

"I know the Bible, but I just can't seem to apply it."

But sometimes he surely acted like a man who *could* read minds! "Only God's grace can help you do that."

"Do you think He's withholding His grace from me?"

"Oh, no! He would never do that—just look at the cross."

"Then why can't I take hold of Him through faith, like you have?"

"I'm not sure. Have you asked Him to help you do this thing?"

"Yes, many times. But it doesn't come."

"My father taught me that God's love and forgiveness pour out freely to everyone from a never-ending fountain. If you've asked but not received, then something must be stopping the flow from reaching you."

"But I wanted it more than anything. I wouldn't knowingly stop it."

"Then you must be stopping it unknowingly. Satan will do anything to keep you away from Jesus. Tricking people is his best act. Remember the Garden of Eden?"

Leroy stared at me with astonishment in his eyes. I could tell such a thought had never occured to him. I wondered then why it had suddenly come to me.

Leroy took a long drink from his coffee mug. I sensed that he needed time to do some serious thinking and praying.

"Have your mother and father been over to your new apartment yet?"

"Yes. Dad came over one night after work. Mom met us there and I cooked dinner for the three of us."

"Michael didn't come?"

"I asked him to, but he said he had other plans. I don't think he really wanted to come anyway. Michael doesn't spend any more time with me than he has to."

I studied the gentle expression on Leroy's face for a minute before I spoke. I couldn't tell by the calm I saw there whether Michael's attitude bothered him or not. Knowing Leroy as I was beginning to, I didn't see how it could not.

"I'm sorry Michael's so...well, so like he is."

"Now you're apologizing for him, and to his own brother."

"I suppose somebody needs to."

"It's almost like not having a brother at all—a real brother, that is," Leroy said softly.

I saw pain cloud his blue eyes then, and I knew he was remembering something in the past, perhaps some long-ago time when things had been different. I guessed that relations had not always been so strained between Leroy and his brother, and I wondered how they had ever gotten that way. I wanted to ask, of course, but the look that had come on Leroy's face kept me from speaking.

Finally he heaved a deep sigh, cleared the memory from his eyes, and spoke. "You said you kept busy growing up without any brothers and sisters, but I know it must have been lonely without a mother."

"It was in a way, I guess, but my father and I did a lot of things together, and there was this wonderful lady who took care of me after school till my father got home from work. It was nice. She took care of the house and the cooking, and she was there for me when I needed someone to talk to."

"She should've taught you how to cook," he said with a playful grin.

"Oh, she did. Well, I learned how to keep a house, but I never liked the cooking part. I was a lousy pupil."

"After I got polio and couldn't do a lot of other things, I started taking more interest in things that didn't take much physical activity. I learned the basics about cooking from watching our housekeeper."

Leroy looked tenderly into my eyes then, and stillness suddenly filled the air between us. "You haven't touched your coffee," he said at length.

"I don't drink coffee."

"But you brought two cups. You brought two cups before, too."

"Just to be sociable, but it really doesn't do a thing for me."

"It doesn't?"

Our eyes had become engrossed and I could tell Leroy wanted to kiss me.

"Robert Redford doesn't either."

"What?"

"I've never gotten over Elvis Presley's smile."

"You know, you're really too young to be an Elvis fan."

"My father said I inherited it from my mother."

"You don't inherit things like that."

How could Leroy sound like Bertha at a time like this?

"You know, Elvis' smile was one-in-a-lifetime, but then there's your—"

Leroy's arms were suddenly around me. He drew me close and touched his lips tenderly on mine. They were soft as the petals of a rose, and his kiss was the sweetest kiss I'd ever known.

Chapter 11

Sunday afternoons on Leroy's boat soon became a habit. We would have lunch after church at his apartment or go out to a nice restaurant. Most of the time Leroy cooked my favorite Chinese dinners. Leroy was a genius in the kitchen; he managed so well in that area and handled his other domestic chores with such expertise that I found it difficult to think of him as disabled.

Sometimes Leroy and I would have Sunday dinner with Mr. and Mrs. Britton at their home, and then hurry down the back lawn and across the dock to the water. Often during the week we would go out to the lake when I wasn't volunteering at the hospital or when Leroy wasn't meeting with his HAL group (though we never went sailing on prayer meeting night). Dinner would always be waiting at the Britton's table when we arrived, prepared scrumptuously by their delightful housekeeper and cook, Mavis. "Song bird" was the meaning of the black woman's name, and she never failed to live up to it, always humming or singing around the kitchen when I was there.

I remember one evening in particular when Leroy and I had come in early from the lake (the wind wasn't strong enough, he had said). Mr. Britton had asked Leroy into the den to discuss a matter of business and Mrs. Britton had gone to a committee meeting at church. That left me in the care of the devoted Mavis, and I took deep pride in following her around the kitchen listening to tales of her first days with the Britton clan. Mavis had come to the Brittons the year Michael was born into the family. That meant she had known Leroy since he was three years old. It gave the black woman much pleasure to recount stories about the boys' early childhood and how Michael had adored his big brother from the time he was old enough to take his first steps.

"It was a sight to see those little fellows rompin' and playin' together," Mavis said. "They were such happy little guys. Leroy was such a good boy, and Michael was, too, but he was a little more rambunctious." She smiled affectionately.

Then Mavis told me about the sadness that gripped the Britton household for a while when Leroy came down with dreaded polio.

"That sweet little child tried so hard," she recounted, "but it didn't do him no good. He was crippled and he couldn't walk no more, didn't matter how hard he tried." A great look of sorrow washed over the black woman's face, and I could tell she was vividly recalling Leroy's long days of pain and struggling. "I don't know why, but things was different between the boys after that. They didn't seem to be as close. Oh, they'd go off to the woods still, and they always played in the woods on the other side of the lake, but they got into a lot of scrapes.

"Leroy started spendin' more time here in the kitchen with me. And it just broke my heart to see that little guy gettin' around on crutches when he'd been such a healthy, fun-lovin' boy. But he wasn't changed none. He was the same sweet, happy little boy he'd always been."

Memory washed over her face again. "Then his daddy got him his first boat. That kid took to the water like a duck. Sailin' took all his spare time after that. I always thought after he grew up he gave his heart to sailin' the way most men give their heart to a woman. What with him being crippled, seems like Leroy thought sailin' was a better way to spend his time than courtin'." She gave me a smile of secret understanding. "Till now, that is."

Before long I grew to love Mavis and also Leroy's parents, and I took much delight in the time spent with them. They became the family I didn't have. I soon came to love the fine art of sailing, too. Leroy and I frequently attended the sailboat regattas held at the yacht club at the south end of Lake Wyeth, and I loved the competition of the race almost as much as he did. Though I didn't have any hope of becoming a master of the craft of sailing that Leroy was, he patiently kept teaching me, and learning at the hand of such an excellent teacher certainly made the task pleasant and easy.

The quiet days and evenings on the clear lake became endearing to my heart and such a source of peace to my soul, partly because of the wonderful young man with whom I was spending so much time. After Steve had met Noreen, I knew my chance to be his girl was gone forever, and I didn't think I'd ever want to be anyone else's girl. I suppose I thought I'd just be alone for the rest of my life. Alone and lonely. But Leroy changed all that. I thought about Steve less and less, mostly just at church when we were all there together or at the hospital when we had a chance to talk. My unknown love for him was something I would always have to live with, but it didn't seem as though it was going to interfere with my life.

Probably the only cloud hovering on my horizon as the beautiful summer moved lazily along was the thought of my writing. After work at the candy shop, I was spending so much time with Leroy that I didn't have any time for one of the things I loved most. I still wasn't sure how God wanted to use me in that area, but I had a distinct feeling that He had something special in mind for me, so I didn't let the slack time trouble me too much. But I knew I needed to write something—anything—if I was to grow in skill. At the end of each day, during my devotion time with the Lord, I began writing "letters" to God, expressing my thoughts and feelings not only verbally but on paper as well. I saved these "letters" in a neat folder which I put in the drawer of the nightstand beside my bed. It wasn't until some time later that these words on paper proved to be an invaluable source to me.

The summer was especially joyous to me because of what took place in Leroy's life. It happened this way.

Since the first time I had mentioned it, we had talked on numerous occasions about God's grace being poured out freely and equally to all who would receive it. We spent many evenings together searching the Scriptures and we spent much time in prayer seeking God's will for Leroy. We prayed earnestly for Leroy's response to the Holy Spirit's call.

It came on a night in late June when Leroy had a meeting with HAL. He said he would come by my apartment afterward for coffee, so I was taking advantage of the time alone to do some reading, a highly regarded pastime of mine and one so helpful to my writing. My favorite music was pouring softly and tenderly from the stereo and Chow Mein was curled up beside me on the couch. The hour had grown late and I decided that Leroy had been held up for unexpected reasons and would not be able to come after all. I knew he would call, nevertheless, and explain his delay no matter how late it became. As I got ready for bed I was listening almost unconsciously for the ringing of the telephone.

The doorbell's chime startled me. I was writing my devotions, but put them quickly aside and hastened to answer it. I found Leroy waiting on the porch, a look on his face I had not seen before. He came inside talking so fast that it was a full ten minutes and two cups of coffee later before he calmed down enough for me to understand what he was saying.

"There wasn't anything different or unusual about the meeting at first," Leroy explained. "There was just the regular group of us and I was addressing the group on some proposals, when out of nowhere it hit me. As I stood before them, I looked around the room and it was like the first time I'd ever seen those people. Some of them were on crutches just like I am, and some were in wheelchairs and some of them had artificial arms or legs. Some of them were blind—a real roomful of freaks, Michael would say." He laughed excitedly. "I stared at all those people and I thought about each of their different situations and it surprised me, but I found myself thinking how much God loved each one of them! They were crippled or blind or had some other physical disability, but God loved them all! Then I thought—and He loves me, too! He really does because nothing that happens to us can separate us from His love! The Scripture says so!

"I still don't know why disabilities have to be endured, but I know that disabilities are part of life like anything else, and they are certainly not of God's doing. I know He's only working for our good. What I'm trying to say is, I really have blamed God all this time for my disability. Satan had been tricking me into thinking that and keeping me from becoming a Christian. He was making me crippled in a way that had nothing to do with my legs.

"You know, Holly, I don't think people realize how much power Satan has. I didn't. Somehow he had me believing that God didn't really love me. But I got to thinking that if He loved everyone else in that room, and I knew He did, then why not me?

"I realized then that God never said we wouldn't have any adversity, but He did say He'd be with us through everything and He'd never leave us. I realized we need not worry about ourselves and our imperfections because God will work out His purposes in us if we yield to Him. But I wouldn't yield—I wanted Him to come to me, but I wouldn't really go to Him. It was like I'd been saying all these years: If You love me, Lord, like I've been told You do, then why did You let me become crippled?

"Well, at that moment everything began to happen. A power came over me and I couldn't go on talking. I was filled with the Holy Spirit and the whole room was suddenly filled. Then I thought of the Scripture in Hebrews 4 that says, 'Let us therefore come boldly unto the throne of grace that we may obtain mercy, and find grace to help in time of need.'

"Right there at the front of the room I went to the throne and received the grace I'd been rejecting. I asked God's forgiveness and took Jesus into my heart as my Lord and Savior. Then I could really claim 1 John 4:4—'Greater is He that is in you than he that is in the world'—meaning Satan. Then the strangest thing happened. I was so filled with the Holy Spirit that I began talking again, only I didn't talk about the proposals. I began sharing my experience and the problem I'd had with God most of my life, or rather, the problem He'd had with me, and right there at the meeting two other people received His grace and accepted Christ as their Savior!''

"Oh, Leroy!" I cried and threw my arms around his neck. He had just been saved and already the Lord had used him to bring two others into the kingdom! Tears rushed unchecked down my face, and Leroy hugged and kissed me again and again. It was the most exciting night of our lives!

The next Sunday Leroy went forward at the morning worship service to make public his commitment to the Lord. He gave the most precious testimony, sharing some of what he'd shared with me, and I couldn't keep from crying all over again.

Chapter 12

It was an afternoon in midsummer when I looked up from the fountain to see Abigail Haysley coming into the shop. She was quite flustered, patting the curls of her immaculate hairdo and tugging at the hem of her tailored jacket. I smiled discreetly as she marched across the floor, for I knew what was coming.

"Holly, I just don't understand it! I've never been stood up in my life!" She flopped her patent leather handbag on the counter. "Mr. Reed and I were to have lunch at that darling little nook around the corner—that new place on the other side of the bank, The Town Cottage. I've been waiting for over an hour, but he hasn't come."

"It's all right, Mrs. Haysley," I explained and glanced across the store at Bertha, who stood behind a candy case watching us with a smug grin on her suntanned face. "Mr. Reed tried to call you at home, but you'd already left for the restaurant. He felt quite bad because he couldn't recall the name of the restaurant. If he could've remembered the name, he would have called you there."

"Well, where is he? What's happened?"

"He went to have some repairs done on his car and got delayed. They promised to have his car finished before noon, but they didn't get to it as soon as they expected. So you see there's a simple explanation and no need for you to get upset."

Mrs. Haysley seemed to calm down a bit.

"He said if I talked to you to convey his apologies and ask if he could make up for lunch by taking you to dinner tonight."

The elderly woman beamed graciously while smoothing the curls of her silver hair and adjusting the slant of her wire glasses. "Well, I suppose that would make up for things. After all, it wasn't his fault."

I looked over at Bertha and winked. She rolled her dark, expressive eyes and turned to busy herself with a nearby display of chocolates. I knew I would hear from her later.

Mrs. Haysley climbed on a tall stool at the fountain. "I might as well have some ice cream," she said, "since I didn't have any lunch. Do you have any lemon sherbet today, dear? Mr. Reed makes the best lemon sherbet in this town."

A busy afternoon kept Bertha from conversing with me for the rest of the day. When Mr. Reed returned, much later, I gave him the message Mrs. Haysley had left. He smiled and went his usual, congenial way back to his office.

I was getting ready to leave when Bertha came up behind the fountain. "Holly, I just don't see how you can be so nice to Abigail Haysley all the time. She gives me a pain right where I sit."

"Oh, Bertha," I laughed, "what's wrong with Mrs. Haysley? She's just a lonely old woman. She and Mr. Reed enjoy each other's company, so what's the harm?"

"She makes me sick the way she patronizes ol' Mr. Reed like he was solid gold or something."

I studied my co-worker thoughtfully, deciding that the only thing wrong with Bertha was that she didn't have anyone to patronize her. "It's nice they've been seeing so much of each other."

"Next thing you know they'll be getting married."

"That's what usually happens."

"Is that what you and Leroy are going to do?"

I was completely taken aback at Bertha's question. "Leroy and me?"

"Yeah. Are you two gonna get married? You've been seeing an awful lot of each other."

"Oh. Well...I don't know. I mean, we don't have any plans of that sort." I wondered why I hadn't given Bertha a flat "No" to her question. I certainly had never considered marriage to Leroy. You had to love a person before you wanted to marry him, at least in most cases, and I was still in love with Steve.

Just then Cara came by and said good night to us. She smiled sweetly and with quickened steps disappeared through the front door.

"She's going to meet Gil, I guess," Bertha said dejectedly.

Gil was Gilbert Thornton, a new salesman who worked across the street at Wingfield's Department Store. He had been keeping steady company with Cara for several weeks. She had even begun bringing him to church.

"Since you helped her fix herself up she sure has changed a lot," Bertha continued.

"The outward change was just a small one—it's what happened to her in the inside that's made the real difference." I gazed levelly at Bertha. "I wish you could experience the change that took place inside Cara."

"What's the matter with the way I am?"

"I didn't mean it that way. Becoming a Christian wouldn't change basically who you are. It would just add a blessing to your life that nothing else could give you."

"You know what I'd really like?"

"What's that?"

Bertha went to get her purse from a drawer under one of the candy cases. I took mine from behind the fountain and we started out. On the sidewalk in front of the store, Bertha lit a cigarette and fastened her dark eyes on me.

"Promise you won't laugh or anything."

"I promise."

"I've been thinking about how you helped Cara, showing her how to put on makeup and fix her hair and all." She took a long puff from her cigarette and blew the smoke forcefully into the air. "Could you help me a little with something like that?"

"Why, I'd be glad to help you."

"What about a diet—do you think I should go on a diet?"

"Well..." I hesitated, studying Bertha avidly. She was almost as tall as Leroy, but I was sure she weighed much more.

"You can tell me. I asked you, didn't I? Oh, you don't have to say anything. I know I need to lose some weight, but it takes so darn much willpower."

"Have you ever thought of asking God to help you with it?"

Bertha laughed her hooting laugh. "Oh, come on, Holly."

"I mean it." I brightened suddenly. "Bertha, I've got a great idea! We've just started a new class in church training on Sunday nights. It's called The Three D Class—Dieting, Discipline, and Discipleship. It would be wonderful for you. The whole concept is to grow in the Lord and lose weight and develop greater willpower. I bet it would help you a lot. You might even get your smoking under better control." I knew I shouldn't have added that last part, but I couldn't help it—the words just flew out. But Bertha didn't seem to mind. I could tell by the expression on her face that she was intrigued with the idea of the class, so I hastened on. "Some really nice young women attend the class; women of all ages go and the teacher is friendly and dedicated. Why don't you give it a try?"

"Are you in the class?"

"No, I'm attending another class right now, but some of my friends are going to the Three D class and they'd be glad for you to come."

"I don't know about that discipleship part."

"It all works together. You'll like it, you'll see. Of course, before you can be a disciple, you have to become a Christian, and I'm praying very hard for you."

Bertha gave me a look that said she thought I was crazy, but she didn't say anything.

"The Three D class starts at 6:30."

"Are there any men in the class?"

I grinned furtively. So Bertha had actually gotten around to saying what was really on her mind. "I don't think so."

"Do a lot of young men go to your church?"

"Yes, some."

"Anybody I might like?"

I shrugged. "Gee, I don't know. What kind of men do you like?" I thought about Michael Britton and cringed inwardly.

"Just the usual type." She paused and looked warily over at me. "But not anybody like Leroy. I'm just not like you and Cara. Say, where is Leroy tonight? Isn't he taking you home?"

"He has a meeting with HAL. What did you mean, you're not like Cara and me?"

"I told you before, I don't go for Leroy's type."

"Gil isn't Leroy's 'type,' as you call it. He doesn't have a physical disability."

"What's Gil got to do with it? Cara was nuts about Leroy before she ever met Gil, back before you came to work here."

"How do you know that?"

"Well, she didn't tell me or anything. Cara hardly ever said anything before, but I could tell how she felt. Leroy was the only one she had anything to do with."

"Did she and Leroy go out?"

Bertha shook her head. "Leroy's never had eyes for anybody around here but you."

"Do you think Cara still feels the same way about him?"

"No, I don't think so. She looks all moon-eyed at Gil now. I think she just liked Leroy 'cause he was so nice to her. I mean, who could really go for a guy like—" She stopped short. "Holly, I'm sorry."

"Bertha, do you have any idea how fortunate we are?"

"What're you talking about?"

"We can do all kinds of tough things—like opening doors and climbing steps."

"Huh?"

"Leroy's a wonderful person. It's not fair to judge him by something so unimportant as the way he walks."

"I'll take his brother any day."

I looked at Bertha and almost laughed. Bertha and Michael? It seemed ludicrous, but then a wild thought struck me. Those two were really quite well-suited for each other. It was kind of like divine justice. They deserved each other. Getting Bertha and Michael together seemed like a good idea. I decided to mention it to Leroy.

We were sitting on my couch later that evening. He laughed his beautiful, sunny laugh. "Playing cupid's a dangerous game, Holly. Besides, Michael's all wrapped up in Linda Benton right now. And every time I see her she's wrapped *around* him."

"Oh? Sounds like there's a lot of things going on at your father's bank besides banking."

Leroy grinned at me. "No, Dad runs a tight ship, but you know how Michael is—there's not much controlling him at times."

"Do you think Michael and Linda are serious?"

"Who can tell about Michael? He's had as many girls as changes of clothes."

"Maybe if Bertha goes on a diet and gets to looking better..."

Leroy tossed his head back and laughed. "It'll take more than a diet."

I couldn't help laughing with him. "We should be ashamed of ourselves," I admonished a minute later.

"But we're not." He slipped his arm around me and pulled me near. "What I should be ashamed of is the thoughts that go through my mind when I'm sitting here alone with you like this."

I looked up as Chow Mein came in from the kitchen. "We aren't alone—there's my cat."

"You should have a mountain lion to protect you from the thoughts I'm thinking."

I studied the calm blue of his eyes and the gentle curve of

his mouth. "I don't need anything to protect me from you."
I smiled mischievously. "You aren't in any condition to cause
a girl any problems."

"That's what you think, Miss Good Luck," he said, taking
me by the arms and pinning my body to the back of the couch.
"The only thing about me that doesn't work is my legs."

I sat motionless beneath his overwhelming strength. Then suddenly he laughed and closed me in his arms. Soon his soft lips
found mine and their tender, sweet taste lingered in my memory
long after he whispered good night at my door.

Chapter 13

⧫⧫⧫⧫⧫⧫

It was not long till closing time on Wednesday when the front door jingled open, admitting Abigail Haysley into the shop. Little did I know on this hot July afternoon that I was about to find out that in spite of her affected manner and accumulated wealth the elderly woman possessed a heart of true goodness. I was only sorry that Bertha missed the whole scene, but she was on the phone in the corner taking a candy order.

Leroy was standing at the end of the fountain drinking a Coke, and I had just finished serving a banana split to a young customer near the door, when Mrs. Haysley came bustling inside inquiring about the time a particular bus was due. I reached under the counter for the bus schedule that Mr. Reed always kept there for the convenience of his customers and his employees.

"I'm sorry, Mrs. Haysley, it looks like you just missed that one. It'll be about 30 minutes before another one comes."

"I didn't miss it, dear. I just got off it," she said almost shyly.

I looked at her as though she had been separated from her better judgment. "You *what?*"

"Well, you see, I caught it up the line a bit. I was doing some shopping at Barksdale's and then I was going out to my sister's in Briarhaven. I thought about taking a taxi, but expenses are rising so much that I feel better being a bit more economical when I can." She smiled discreetly.

"But why did you get off the bus?"

"Well," she went on even more timidly than before, which wasn't at all like Abigail Haysley, "there was this terribly crippled young man on the bus. He got on a little after I did, but nobody offered him a seat. I knew he would be embarrassed if an old lady like me got up for him, so I just pretended it was time for me to get off..." She stopped suddenly and stared down toward the end of the fountain where Leroy stood. Then a bright crimson color crept over her face, and I knew she hadn't noticed him before. But she went on limply, "...and I rang the bell to get off just as he was alongside my seat. In that way I know he wasn't embarrassed...and you know, there's always another bus."

Mrs. Haysley grasped the edge of the marble fountain to steady herself, and I thought for a minute she was going to pass out. The color had drained entirely from her face and she had turned as pale as newborn snow.

"Oh, Holly...oh, goodness, I didn't mean to...oh, what have I said?"

I glanced down the fountain at Leroy, but he was already making his way to Mrs. Haysley, a sunny smile on his face. He came to a stop at her side and, letting his crutches hang from his arms, he took her small, creased hands and held them tenderly in his large, strong ones.

"I think what you did was the kindest, most understanding gesture I've ever heard of anyone making. Thank you for taking time out of your day to really care."

Mrs. Haysley smiled not so prudently this time and I saw a teardrop, ever so tiny, roll onto her powdered cheek. She brushed it hurriedly away and then went up on tiptoe and kissed Leroy on the side of the face. "I must confess, Leroy, when I saw that other young man with his legs so crippled like yours, I thought about you, and I wondered if he could be as fine a person as you are. I hope so."

Leroy leaned over and brushed Mrs. Haysley's cheek with a grateful kiss. I could tell that he was beyond putting his feelings into any further words.

"Well, I must go," she clucked, smiling cheerfully again. "I'll just have time to run over to Wingfield's for a few minutes before that other bus comes."

When Mrs. Haysley had gone, Leroy looked after her for a long time. He never spoke of the incident again, but I knew he had been deeply moved by her display of compassion, perhaps too moved to express it to any greater extent. Leroy was beginning to teach me that many of life's most beautiful and tender moments were inexpressible in mere human words and gestures.

Reviewing the incident with Abigail Haysley caused me to think of Bertha's critical attitude toward the woman. I made a point of telling her about the occurrence on the bus.

"So you see," I concluded, "people aren't always what they seem—good or bad." The words had no sooner left my mouth than I thought of Michael Britton.

Friday afternoon Linda Benton came bouncing into the shop. I made her a cherry soda and she climbed onto a red leather stool and sat drinking and talking. Bertha and Cara were busy with candy customers, so Linda kept me occupied with a few tales of interest from the loan department of the bank and a few comments about the hot weather.

Later, when Linda was about to leave, she jumped down from her stool and then suddenly turned her brown velvet eyes on me. "Holly, I don't know what you've done to Leroy, but he's sure been acting strange these days."

"Strange?"

She tossed aside a long blonde curl. "Well, he smiles all the time. Course he did that a lot before, but he's different now. He talks a lot about religious things and he keeps saying stuff about being 'born again.' At first I didn't think he had both his oars in the water, but he's really sincere. And he's got a way about him, you know? He's got a way of explaining things that really makes you want to listen to what he says. I don't know what you've done to him, but there seems to be a better spirit of things around our department these days."

I smiled at Linda, rejoicing inwardly. I knew that the Holy Spirit was having His way in Leroy's life, and I silently thanked God again for what He had done. It was right then that I decided to prepare a little surprise for Leroy.

"Well, I have to get back to work," Linda was saying. "I don't want to get in trouble with my boss." She laughed with a lighthearted gleam in her brown eyes.

"Oh, Linda, would you do me a favor?" I called as she

started across the floor. "Would you give your boss a message? Tell him not to come by for me after work. Tell him just come on over to my apartment around 7:30. And tell him not to eat."

"Sure, Holly. See you later."

When Leroy arrived I was in the kitchen. I had had such delightful plans—I thought. But the delight had turned into a disaster. Most of the smoke had cleared by the time I went to answer Leroy's ring, but the odor would remain for some time to come.

"What happened, the place catch on fire?"

He was joking, but I only stared frantically at him and burst into tears. The grin dissolved on his face and he sought to comfort me in his arms. He propped his crutches against the wall nearby and reached gently for me, but I turned abruptly and went back to the kitchen. Leroy retrieved his crutches and followed.

The room was a shambles. Burned pans sat on the stove, accumulated dishes lay piled in the sink, and an array of mixes and spices cluttered the counter tops. Out of the entire fiasco stood one spark of hope—the table in the dining area. It was set with my best china and crystal along with a cluster of blue candles and flowers set in a lovely, delicate arrangement in the center.

I looked pitifully at Leroy as he came to my side. He stood there a minute as if to reassure himself that I wasn't going to run away again, then he propped his crutches against a nearby cabinet and began gently brushing the tears from my cheeks. I reached up and held his hands there against my face—such fine, strong hands that served him so well. Then he tilted my chin up so I was looking into his face. Smiling, he said, "What were you trying to do?"

"I wanted to surprise you. I was cooking dinner for you. It

was supposed to be a sort of celebration of your new Christian life, and I wanted to do it anyway because you've cooked so many dinners for me.''

Leroy looked so sweetly at me that I thought I was going to cry again, but suddenly his lips tenderly claimed mine and I forgot all about cooking and kitchens and burned dinners.

Minutes later we stood looking at the mess. "I should have stuck to what I know best," I offered. "I should have stuck to the only thing I know about in the kitchen—making Chinese dinners. But we have them so often. I wanted to make something different for you. You said you really liked Italian food, so I thought why not give it a try. I've got this great cookbook that my old maid aunt in Virginia gave me. She said—"

"Holly."

"Yes."

"Hush, you're babbling."

Suddenly I shook with laughter. "I'm sorry. I'm not usually a babbler. Outspoken, yes. But I suppose there's not much you can say when you've practically burned down the kitchen."

"Why don't we clean up the mess?"

"Oh, no, I'll do that later."

Leroy was at the sink before I could stop him. He began clearing the dishes into the dishwasher and then drew water to soak the scorched pans.

"How did this happen, anyway?"

I brought him the pans from the range. "Actually things probably wouldn't have been so bad, but after I put everything in the oven to bake I went in the living room and sat down to review a story I'd been working on a while back. I got all engrossed in what I was doing and forgot all about what I had cooking till I smelled it and saw the smoke. I guess I had the fire up too high, but I thought it would get done faster."

Leroy let out a long, exasperated sigh. "You better stick to writing from now on."

"I promise."

"Now, why don't you get out of here and let me fix us something to eat."

"Fix is what you'll have to do all right."

"What?"

"Repair, that's what fix means, but you'll have to do better than that. You'll have to improvise."

"Just get out of here and let me *prepare* us something to eat."

"Or *cook* us something."

"I don't need a grammar lesson right now."

"I sure could use a lesson in cooking."

"Not now."

"This whole thing is my fault. At least let me help. What will you cook? Let's see, there's some more hamburger in the fridge and some packages of different stuff up there in the cabinet and a few canned goods, too. I've got salad ingredients in the fridge, too. I was going to make tossed salad after I finished reading over my story, but I didn't exactly get around to it. Why don't I make the salad while you whip us up something out of the hamburger?"

"You're babbling again."

"I'm not."

"Do you know how to make a *good* salad?" he said, as though he thought I were some kind of idiot. I glanced around the kitchen. Maybe he was right.

"Sure. I've watched you. There's nothing to it. You just cut it all up and toss it together. That's where they get the name, isn't it? You just toss it all together—that's a snap."

Leroy rolled his calm eyes. "Try not to burn it, okay?"

"How could I burn salad?"

"It wouldn't surprise me if *you* found a way."

I made a grotesque face at him on my way to the refrigerator. I got out the salad greens and Leroy pretended not to pay any attention to what I was doing, but I knew he was watching me out of the corner of his eye. He doesn't trust me, I thought. Well, I sure hadn't given him any reason to.

All went well as I washed the vegetables—carrots, radishes, green peppers, celery, cucumbers, tomatoes, and a small onion. I had just finished washing the lettuce and had picked up a knife when out of nowhere Leroy was at my side, a look of horror on his face.

"What are you going to do with that knife?"

"I'm not going to kill anybody. I'm just going to cut up the lettuce."

"You don't cut lettuce with a knife."

"Well, what do you cut it with?"

"You don't cut it."

"But I've seen you do it."

"No, you haven't. You've seen me chop up the other vegetables, but you don't cut lettuce. You tear it."

"Why?"

"The metal knife blade will make the edges of the lettuce turn brown. Here, you tear it like this." He took the head of lettuce and broke it into several chunks, then began tearing the leaves very gently into pieces.

"That could take half the night."

"No, it won't. Why don't you run on in the living room and let me take care of this. Go put on some music or something."

I looked up disapprovingly at him. "You're talking to me like I was a little girl."

"Well, you're not very big."

"You know what I mean."

"Go listen to the golden tones of your music, and let me do this."

The thought was tempting, but my ego was bruised. I needed a chance to prove myself something other than a clown in the kitchen. (I don't know why that was so important to me. I couldn't have cared less about the kitchen. I suppose it was because of Leroy. I didn't want him to think I was so dumb.)

"This was supposed to be my treat to you. At least let me make the salad, let me *try* to make the salad. And you can help me if I run into any more trouble."

He smiled a bright, reassuring smile. "Okay."

A short time later my kitchen looked respectable again, and on the dining table sat a hamburger/rice casserole, French green beans, tossed salad, and large French rolls that Leroy had gotten hurriedly at a delicatessen down the block.

I gazed across the table at Leroy.

"Thank you for coming to my rescue in the kitchen."

"I didn't come to your rescue. You had the fire out by the time I got here."

I laughed. "You know what I mean. Dinner is delicious."

"Your salad makes the whole meal."

"Sure."

"It's good. You might make a hand in the kitchen yet."

"I'd rather watch you."

He grinned affably. "I'd rather you watched me, too."

After dinner we were sitting on the couch in the living room and Leroy was having coffee. We were talking and watching TV now and then, when Leroy took notice of the stack of papers resting on the corner of the glass coffee table.

"Is that the story you were reading before the kitchen went up in smoke?"

"Yes," I said, laughing easily.

"Would you object if I looked at it?"

"I wouldn't mind at all—in fact, I'd appreciate your opinion, but I don't think my stories would interest a man. They're really geared for young women."

"Has anyone ever given you a critique—other than the publishers, I mean?"

"They don't give you much critique. They almost always just send a form rejection notice. Very rarely do they make a comment. I know how busy they are and how many manuscripts cross their desks every day, so even a word or two is encouraging. At least I know what I've done hasn't been a total waste. Once I got a note from an editor saying he couldn't use the particular story I'd sent him, but he would be glad to consider more of my work in the future. I can't tell you how encouraging that was. I feel like if I keep writing, sooner or later I'll get published. Sometimes I think the hardest part is finding the right market at the right time."

"Have you thought about getting an agent?"

"Yes, many times, but that can be as difficult as finding the right publisher. And I don't think many agents take on writers who haven't had at least one piece of work published, unless you happen to be one of those rare geniuses. And there isn't anyone like that around here."

Leroy picked up my manuscript, glancing casually over it. "Are you sure? Maybe you underestimate your ability."

"No, I don't, but I don't overstate it either."

"You didn't tell me—has anyone read your work?"

"No one but Steve—" It was out before I could stop. And I knew I reddened because Leroy surveyed my face skeptically. "And...and my father," I finished haltingly. "They've read just a few of my manuscripts. And my teachers have read some."

"What did they say about them?"

"They were encouraging. Of course my father only read some of my first work, and he pointed out what he thought were some weak areas. I believe I'm improved in those areas, too. I've been working at it, trying to develop my style and skill. But really I think style comes out naturally. I just write what I feel and the way I feel it, and I can see my style emerging."

"What did Steve say?" Leroy asked, his blue eyes almost burning a hole through me.

"He says I write very well—effectively, he calls it." I started to laugh. "You know, it's funny—my stories are written for women, but only men have read them so far, except for the editors at the magazine publications. Some of them were women."

"May I take this story home?"

"Yes, if you like, and I'll be anxious to know what you think of it."

"I'll let you know soon." He returned my manuscript to the coffee table, then leaned back and slipped his arm around me. "Would you like to go somewhere kind of special with me next Saturday?"

"What's the special occasion?"

"It's not really a special occasion—just a special fellowship that HAL is having at the community center. We'll have dinner and music and a time for activities and fellowship—just a big party."

"Sounds like fun. What time shall I be ready?"

"I'll pick you up early, about 6:30."

Chapter 14

We were on our way to the HAL fellowship when we drove past a big intersection not far from the community center. A group of men were erecting a gigantic canvas tent on a corner lot. A large sign nearby offered an explanation of their activities:

CRUSADE FOR CHRIST
EVANGELISTIC SERVICE AND FAITH HEALING
The Rev. Maynard P. Burnside, Officiating
August 22-29
Seven-thirty Each Evening
Come and bring a lost or afflicted friend!

"Have you ever been to one of those?" asked Leroy.

"No, but I've heard about them and I've seen them on TV."

"Do you believe things like that really happen—the faith healing, I mean?"

"I've heard so much about the phonies connected with it that I'm afraid it affects my opinion."

"The disciples healed in Jesus' name. Do you think people really do it today?"

"I don't know. I believe it's possible. I believe if a person has enough faith anything can happen, and I believe there are people today who have that kind of faith. I just don't know if mine is that strong."

That was all Leroy said about the crusade at that time. It was more than three weeks away, and I all but forgot about it long before then.

What I didn't forget about—ever—was my writing. Leroy had returned my manuscript the next day after he had taken it home. He had agreed that it was aimed at young women and he had praised it highly. His encouragement was really a boost to my precarious ego, and his assurance that it was only a matter of time till God led me further in my efforts caused me to even more earnestly seek the Lord's will for my life. There was no way that Leroy or I could have known that God would answer my prayers so quickly.

At the HAL fellowship, Leroy introduced me to many of his wonderful friends. The sensitivity and warmth of the people I met was overwhelming, and the evening was one of the most enjoyable I had ever spent and one I would not forget. I found myself hoping Leroy would invite me to more of the group's social activities. When I mentioned this to him later, he seemed so pleased.

It was toward the end of the evening that I encountered a

darling little old lady named Johanna Sullivan. Johanna was a Hebrew name and it meant "God's gracious gift." At first I didn't know that Johanna was to be a gracious gift from God to me. I had been struggling for some time with whether God wanted to use me to write for Him. I hadn't been satisfied with my secular stories sent to some of the most popular women's magazines. I believed that God wanted more from me than that. I believed He wanted me to write stories that would share a witness with other people. I had written a few short stories aimed at Christian magazines, but, like the other stories, none had been accepted. More and more I was beginning to think that God wanted me to attempt to write book-length stories, either novels or perhaps some nonfiction work.

Johanna Sullivan was blind. She had lost her sight to painful glaucoma in her early forties. To have had the precious blessing of sight for probably half your life and then to lose it—I could not imagine such a plight of heartache and the ordeal of such an adjustment. But Johanna had taken it in her stride.

I had been talking to her for a little while before I became aware of the door that God was opening for me. Johanna (she graciously insisted that I call her by her first name from the onset of our meeting) was a Christian, and what a living testimony to God she was! An accomplished woman in her field, her secretarial skills had to far outrank those of any of us who could merely type and take dictation and file. Johanna had worked for several prominent businessmen and lawyers during her 70-odd years, and in addition to that she had traveled in her work as well as her leisure. She had met many famous dignitaries and other noted persons, had visited a number of foreign countries, and had seen many sights of grandeur before losing her sight completely. Her work and travel never slowed after her loss. Only recently had she cut her schedule to have more time to devote to HAL, she told me.

Johanna had never married, although she maintained a close association with three young nieces and one or two nephews, thus accounting in part for her beautifully outrageous view of life. It soon became obvious how she so naturally shared her witness with all those who crossed her path. I was later to learn about some of the people won to the Lord through this lovely, timeless woman, but I knew I would never know the countless seeds she had planted.

I sat beside that dear old lady and marveled! She was virtually a walking textbook of life, and, I discovered, there was more than one book stirring around inside her snow-white head. The people she had met and the traveling she had done were enough to fill volumes!

It was when I asked Johanna how she would thank God for the gift of sight that the idea to write her life story came to me.

She felt for my hand and took it sweetly in hers. "Some people use their eyes only to look, but they never really see. They only look and criticize. But a person should thank God by using his eyes to see the good in people. He," she smiled slowly, "or *she* should use their eyes to laugh and smile and express love and forgiveness, and to see what people don't really want to see—the other side of life—the hurting, the loneliness, the ugly, the unlovable. And then maybe a person could thank God by using his eyes to look for a way to help."

"I want to tell your story to the world!" The words tumbled out before I realized my mouth was moving. I squeezed Johanna's hand and smiled a smile she couldn't see.

Johanna was thrilled! She said that such an idea had been floating around in her head for many years and that she had been keeping notes for a long time and had many photographs of places she had been and people she had met. She said her hope had been to someday incorporate all this into a book that would give her testimony to all those with whom she could not come in direct contact.

Johanna cemented my decision to begin work on her life story when she told me that she had encountered several outstanding writers throughout her career and that one in particular had impressed her, but it seemed the two never quite found the time to get together. I was convinced that our meeting was an act of God and I told her so. I told her of my struggle to find God's will for my life in writing and that I felt He had something special in mind for me.

Johanna's blind eyes focused fully on me. "Could it be that the Lord has sent you to me for this reason?"

"I'm sure of it! Although I'm just as sure I'm not as qualified as some other writers you've met. You see, I've never been published."

"Nonsense! You're a writer, aren't you?"

I nodded eagerly, and when she sat waiting patiently, I realized my mistake and added hastily, "Yes, yes, I am!"

"We must plan some time together so we can get to know each other better, and you must bring some of your work over and read it to me."

On Monday morning I spoke to Mr. Reed about my meeting with Johanna Sullivan. We discussed my morning schedule and it was decided that I could do the necessary work for him in the office during three mornings of the week if I doubled my work load. This wouldn't be any problem because I often worked at a leisurely pace during those hours.

The new schedule left me three mornings each week in which to visit Johanna at her home and begin work on her book. I was so excited and thanked God for the opportunity each night during my devotion time. Leroy was happy too, and he listened tirelessly as I recounted my experiences of those mornings. There was so much to tell. Johanna had lived enough for two or three lives!

Though Johanna lived in a small, modest house in a comfortable suburb, her home was beautifully decorated inside and out, and each day I looked forward to working with her in such pleasant surroundings. Our work went along smoothly, and from time to time it occurred to me that if I quit my job at Mr. Reed's shop I could devote more time to her book. My earnings were not great at the shop, but I didn't need even that amount because of my trust fund. I discussed the matter with Leroy and we sought God's guidance. After some deliberation, I decided to stay on at the shop and continue the same work schedule with Johanna. I so enjoyed the work at Mr. Reed's store and felt I wanted to go on being a witness there. Johanna, too, was involved in other activities and our part-time schedule worked well for her.

As the days passed, Johanna grew increasingly dear to me, and my efforts seemed to please her, for she encouraged and praised me lavishly. Telling her story was God's will for me, I knew, and beyond that, she was beginning to fill the need in my life for the mother I couldn't remember and the grandmothers I never knew. With Mr. Reed in the dual role of father and grandfather, and the affection of Leroy's family—most of all, Leroy—my life was completely happy.

How was I to know that disaster and heartache lay just around the corner?

Chapter 15

It was a Wednesday evening near mid-August. Leroy and I sat in my living room. We had just come from prayer meeting, and Leroy was drinking a cup of coffee and I was enjoying a glass of Pepsi.

"Mom and Dad are having a big party this weekend," Leroy said. "They especially want you to be there. It's going to be a family affair. I think it's primarily in honor of us."

"In honor of us?"

"I guess my family thought I might never have a girl, probably partly because of my disability. I know Michael's thought that anyway, even if Mom and Dad haven't. Anyway, this is a special party." He set his brown mug on the coffee table and stared at it a long moment. "I want you to know the real reason I've never had a steady girlfriend," he said, turning to me. "I've dated some, but I've never had girls breaking down my door. I don't kid myself—with a disability like mine I know I'm not all that appealing to women."

"Oh, but you are. You're very appealing—"

"Oh, come on, what could be appealing about a man dragging half his body around everywhere he goes?"

"It doesn't have anything to do with that. It's the person you are."

"You really mean that?" he asked almost shyly.

"Of course I do. The only thing that matters is Leroy, not how Leroy gets around."

"The reason I've never had a steady girl is that I've never met anyone I wanted to be with all the time till I met you."

He closed me in his powerful arms and his gentle lips caught mine, softly, lovingly. "My precious Holly, you're so lovely and sweet." He stroked my long hair and cupped his hands under my chin. "Could you really care for me?"

My arms went up tenderly around his neck. "I care very much," I whispered, and our eyes held in a deep gaze of affection. "Leroy, has anyone ever told you how handsome you are?" I said in a minute.

"You mean besides my mother?"

We grinned at each other and I knew he was joking.

"You are, you know."

"Thank you. But I thought you liked the Elvis type, dark and—"

"There's no such thing as the Elvis *type;* God only made one like him."

"You're crazy," he laughed, and kissed me again.

"Besides," I said a minute later, "Elvis was really fair, like you. He dyed his hair."

"Why did he do that?" he asked in his Bertha-like fashion.

"Oh, he had his reasons...but I guess they don't matter now. I guess a lot of things don't matter now."

• • •

The Britton family gathering was a spectacular affair held outside on the shaded patio overlooking the splendid blue water of Lake Wyeth. It was a balmy afternoon of gentle breezes and clear skies, and I met so many Britton aunts, uncles, and cousins that I lost track of them all. But everyone was as kind and gracious as I assumed any relatives of Leroy's would be.

Michael was, as usual, the only dark spot in the day, but fortunately he didn't stay for the duration. He and Linda Benton left early for what Michael termed "a much more important engagement." By the looks on their faces, I could easily discern what the "engagement" was—a little tete-a-tete at either his apartment or hers—and I would have wagered my integrity that there wouldn't be much talking going on.

That night Leroy and I sat in my living room discussing the events of the day, when suddenly I found myself bringing Michael into the conversation. "There's another side to your brother that most people don't know about, isn't there?"

"What do you mean?"

"Like today when he was playing with those nephews and the way he acted with old Aunt Millie. I saw a different side of him in the candy shop one day, too." I told Leroy about the day Michael had collided with Cara and her packages. "The Michael I saw for those few minutes and the Michael I saw for a little while today aren't the same person I see most of the time."

"I don't know anymore," Leroy said more to himself than to me. "But I think Michael was surprised to see you with me today."

"Why should that surprise him? He knows we've been dating all summer."

"I don't know," Leroy answered, but the look on his face told me a different story. "I guess his pride was hurt when you started dating me instead of him."

"He'll recover—I hope."

"I think that's one reason why he left early today."

"Linda Benton was another reason. And you made him look like a fool, too. I'm glad you did after what he said."

"You mean when he asked you to go dancing?"

"Yes, and in front of everyone like that. Why does he want to hurt you?"

"He can't hurt me—not anymore."

I stared at Leroy for a minute. I believed what he said was true, but I sensed that deep down there was a hurt somewhere from sometime long ago. "What you told him was beautiful."

"That if you went dancing, it'd be with me?"

I smiled. "Yes."

"It wasn't very original."

"It got your point across."

Leroy laughed his invigorating laugh, and Chow Mein put in an appearance, rubbing his sleek body against my legs, then soliciting a gentle pat from Leroy before departing for the bedroom.

I gazed contemplatively at Leroy. "Mavis told me one time that you and Michael used to be so close. How long has he been so cruel to you?"

He gave me a half-smile. "He could be pretty testy when we were kids. Course we were just kids."

"Why does he have the attitude toward you that he does?"

"Being the youngest in the family, Michael received a lot of attention, but then we both did. I'm sure it was always fairly divided. But after I got polio, Mom and Dad were a little more involved with me for some time. They didn't neglect Michael in any way—in fact, I think they went out of their way to see that he received plenty of attention—but I think what happened was the abrupt change of circumstances for a while. I required more time and attention, especially at the very first, when I had to have help with my exercises. Michael seemed to resent it and I don't think he ever got over it."

"Didn't he seem to care about what had happened to you?"

"I think so at first, as much as he could, but he was only eight when it happened and he didn't really understand. Maybe he would have if he had been the older brother and I was the one who tagged along and looked up to him. But it was the other way around, and I think that somehow Michael felt like I'd let him down. I think he was a little ashamed of me in front of his friends, too. He couldn't seem to accept what had happened, and he's never accepted me as a person, either."

Leroy shook his head. "The things he used to do to me, you wouldn't believe."

"What kinds of things?"

"He teased me and called me names a lot. His favorites were 'the cripple,' 'the freak,' and 'the monster.' "

"That must have made you feel terrible."

"It did at first, but after a while it didn't bother me. He did so many other things that name-calling was nothing. We used to love to play in the woods on the other side of the lake. Mavis would pack us a lunch and sometimes we'd go and stay all day.

"After I got polio, going to the woods wasn't so much fun for Michael anymore because I couldn't do a lot of things like

I could before. So Michael started going to the woods for a different reason. We'd go down there, then when we got way into the woods where nobody could see us, Michael would push me down and run off with my crutches so I couldn't go anywhere. Sometimes he'd be gone all day and leave me there without any way to get out.''

"Oh, Leroy, how could he do such a horrible thing?"

"It was his idea of fun, I guess. He'd go off and play with some of his friends and then come back and get me when it was time to go home.''

"What did you do all day while he was gone?"

"There was this one clearing where an old tree stump sat. I'd pull myself up and sit on it and play with sticks and rocks and just fool around. I was well-acquainted with the woods and I liked being there. I watched the birds and animals. I entertained myself. I knew I might as well, since there wasn't any way I could get out, because the underbrush was so thick. I tried several times, but I always got tangled up. I knew my way around, but I just couldn't get around very well without crutches. So I accepted his pranks for what they were and tried to make the best of the situation. When you've been through a bat bout with something like polio, I guess acceptance of things comes easier.''

"Yes, I guess so,'' I replied thoughtfully.

"A few times Michael and I wouldn't go down to the woods till late in the day, and he'd leave me there till after dark. I got pretty scared a couple of times. I thought maybe Michael would go home and say he didn't know where I was and nobody would ever find me. I tell you I was one scared little boy.''

One scared little *crippled* boy, I thought, and looked at Leroy with an aching in my heart at the injustice of what his brother had done. "Didn't you ever tell your parents?"

"I was afraid to. Michael said if I ever told them he'd beat me up. He would've done it, too. After I caught on to what he was doing, I refused to go with him anymore.

"One morning we were in my room and I told him I was never going to the woods with him again. He shoved me down on the bed and started hitting me in the stomach with his fists. He hit me so hard so many times that I got sick and threw up all over the bedspread."

I looked aghast at Leroy. It was hard for me to believe what he was saying, even with what I knew of Michael.

"I was a fairly sturdy kid, too. The therapy I'd gone through in learning how to walk with braces had made me pretty strong, but Michael was strong, too. And I guess I was a little afraid of him. He was about my size then and later he passed me up a little."

"It sounds to me like Michael had more than a jealousy or resentment problem. I think he was a little sick in the head. Maybe he still is."

"I've wondered about that a few times, but I don't really think so. He could've done much worse things. I think he was just acting out what he couldn't understand."

"But why didn't he outgrow it?"

"He did. When he became a teenager, he didn't have much time for me anymore."

"But his attitude hasn't changed."

"I've wondered about that, too, but I don't know the answer."

"He's sick."

"Not really—not sick like you mean. He's got some real personality problems, though."

"Leroy, could I ask you something very personal?"

"Sure."

"Do you love your brother?"

"Sure I love him, and I'd do anything for him. I just wish I knew what to do."

"Don't you feel any resentment or anger toward him for the things he did to you?"

"I can't. I got angry at the time, but I couldn't go on feeling that way. Actually, I felt sorry for Michael. I still do."

I tried to give Leroy an understanding smile, but inside I was seething. At that moment I could have taken Michael Britton apart piece by piece. "I know I shouldn't feel this way, but I wish Michael had gotten polio instead of you."

"Don't say that—you don't really mean it. You wouldn't want anybody to go through that, not even Michael. If it had to happen in our family, it was better for it to happen to me."

I stared at Leroy. I could have cried. "How can you say that?"

"Michael would've had a much harder time handling it. He was always more outgoing than I was. Sometimes it was all he could do to sit still. As a kid I was always more content to do quiet things, but Michael had to be out playing somewhere. He would've died if he couldn't run and tear about."

Suddenly Leroy reached for me. Then, holding me gently in his arms, he said, "I worked it all out when I was a kid. And now I have you. And you make everything all right for me as a man. It doesn't seem to bother you that I'm crippled, and I can't tell you how good that makes me feel. As long as you feel this way, as long as I know you care, it doesn't really matter what Michael does."

Leroy touched my lips with a soft, warm kiss. "Being with you like this, how can anything hurt me?"

Leroy's eyes searched reassuringly for mine, but I couldn't meet his gaze. His words had made me realize our relationship had progresed further than I had intended for it to, and I couldn't help but wonder what Leroy would do if he knew of the love deep in my heart for another man. Thoughts of this sent such a tremble through my heart that I didn't know what to say or do, so I thought to change the subject of conversation.

"Did Michael go to church when you were kids?"

"Oh, sure. We all went."

"Have you ever tried to talk to him about the way things are between the two of you?"

"Things really aren't bad between us all the time. Michael doesn't constantly make cracks, just..."

"Most of the time?"

He nodded. "I tried to talk to him once when we were in high school, but I didn't get anywhere. He actually seemed worse for a while afterward. I couldn't figure it out, but I didn't really try to talk to him anymore after that. Something occurred to me then, though."

"What was that?"

"Well, I may be way off base, but it crossed my mind that Michael just might have felt bad about some of the things he'd said and done, and when I tried to bring them into the open and talk them out, maybe that made him feel worse."

I gazed thoughtfully at Leroy. Finally I said, "You know, you might be right."

I think it was just then that the idea of confronting Michael began to take form somewhere in the dark recesses of my brain.

Leroy continued, "It's common knowledge that we take out our hurts on those we love the most. Maybe Michael's actions fit in there somewhere. There are a lot of common denominators in human nature, but at the same time human nature is so complex that there can be many variations of behavior in each one of us.''

"Has Michael ever accepted Christ as his Savior?''

"Yes, when he was 12, but sometimes I think it was a kind of automatic thing, like I did, because he's never taken an interest in the things of the Lord. But that's unfair for me to say. I'm judging him when I do that.''

I nodded, agreeing absently, because my thoughts were far off. If what Leroy said was true, that Michael really wasn't sick in the head, then perhaps if someone were to talk to him, to become a sort of relief valve for his pent-up emotions.... On the other hand, if someone tried to talk to him and he did have more than just some personality flaws....

Chapter 16

I had just come back from my lunch break. The shop was quiet for a Saturday afternoon. Before long the door jingled open and I looked up expectantly. It was about time for Leroy. He usually put in only a half day at the bank on Saturday, then he came in the shop to talk to me and eat a hot fudge sundae. But the jingling of the front door only brought Cara a candy customer.

I busied myself checking the syrup holders and filling the Coke machine. I was still at this chore when the door of the shop opened again. I glanced up. Steve came inside, his handsome face bright with eagerness. What an unexpected surprise! Then it happened. I surged with a thrill I hadn't felt in months. Seeing Steve when I hadn't planned on it threw my well-guarded feelings off balance, and I knew the trouble deep in my heart was a long way from being over.

If I hadn't expected to see Steve, I certainly wasn't prepared for what he had come to tell me. I suppose I knew it was inevitable, but I just hadn't let myself think that far ahead.

Steve smiled his steady, perfect smile and slid onto a tall stool in front of me. He glanced about the shop. "This sure is a beautiful place, isn't it? I'd heard a lot about it even before you came to work here, but this is the first time I've ever been in here." He turned back to me then, and the expression on his face was so bright with happiness and anticipation that it made my heart pound.

"I know I'll see you tomorrow at church," he said, "but I couldn't wait to tell you the news! I'm on my way over to Noreen's now. Holly, guess what? Noreen and I are getting married in October!"

I should have been able to handle Steve's news better than I did, because deep inside I truly was happy for him. I loved him with all my heart and I wanted him to have what he wanted in life even if it didn't include me. But at that moment it was difficult for me to exude my joy. My sudden thrill at seeing Steve faded. It was all I could do to force a smile. Maybe if the wedding wasn't going to be quite so soon. October was only a month away! I faked my feelings and stood there ridden with guilt. All I could think about was the joyous expression on Steve's face, and how it had been put there by someone else.

"We wanted to have the wedding during the Christmas holidays," Steve went on, "but there's a conflict with some of Noreen's family who live out of town. They can't be here then and she especially wants a favorite aunt and uncle to attend. We talked about getting married the Thanksgiving weekend, but everything seems to work out best for everybody if we have it late next month.''

I was congratulating Steve and listening to further details of his and Noreen's plans when I looked up to see Leroy coming into the shop. I hurriedly extended my phony smile.

Both Steve and Leroy had come to know me quite well, and I'd decided that I must be easy to read anyway, but Steve was far too occupied with the particulars of his upcoming marriage to notice my attitude. I could tell, however, that Leroy immediately sensed that something was wrong. It was about this time that Steve launched into his good news again with Leroy, and I stood grinning at them and feeling like the world's biggest hypocrite.

After Steve left I couldn't face Leroy. He had gone to stand at the end of the fountain and I had moved over to the Coke machine. I just knew that if he could examine my expression he would somehow be able to see clear into the depths of my soul and read my inmost feelings. The man I loved was getting married to someone else, and though I wished the best for him, thoughts of Steve's wedding hurt more than I ever believed anything could hurt.

Since I couldn't meet Leroy's constant gaze, I mumbled something to him about having to finish a chore. He called for me to fix him a Coke as soon as I finished filling the machine.

I took a long time in drawing Leroy's Coke. How could I face him with such trouble in my heart? I knew he wasn't fooled. I just didn't know how much he thought was wrong. Steve's timing had certainly been completely wrong. Why did he have to come to the shop at almost the same time as Leroy? I needed some space to compose myself and get a grip on my emotions again. I mustn't let Leroy know how I felt. It would hurt him deeply.

I stood holding Leroy's Coke and gazing out the front window. Outside the fine, sunny weather had turned bleak and gloomy. I had felt warm, muggy air gush in the door and over the fountain as Steve left the shop, and now the sky was a dismal gray and rain was beginning to fall. What a parallel to my own feelings, I thought.

I must have gazed at the soft drops longer than I realized, for I heard Leroy call my name in his sweet, flowing voice. The sound of it was like a soothing ointment to a gaping wound. The gaping wound was in my heart, but I knew I had to go to him.

I set Leroy's Coke in front of him on the fountain and tried to smile.

"What were you doing down there so long?" he pointedly asked.

I couldn't tell him, I just couldn't! He was so dear to me and he didn't deserve this. I silently begged the Lord to help me spare his feelings.

"I was watching the rain. It's such a contrast from the heat and sun this morning."

Leroy questioned me with his eyes, and I saw doubt flicker in their clear blue. He didn't believe me! Then I saw something else. He didn't believe me, but he wanted to!

The front door opened then, and Michael and Linda Benton came scurrying in from the cool, pouring rain. A sudden chill came over me as I moved to wait on them. When Michael approached the fountain, he appeared ready to have a field day tossing insults at his brother, and I noticed something in Leroy that I hadn't noticed before. He seemed to turn almost involuntarily from Michael's piercing glare as though he secretly dreaded the words that were about to come. Perhaps it was only the timing, I mused. Michael had arrived when emotions were uncertain between Leroy and me, and all Leroy needed was a few insults to add to his already precarious feelings.

But instead of carrying on in his usual cruel and disgusting manner, Michael spoke quite civilly to his brother, then greeted me nonchalantly and ordered two milkshakes. It occurred to me while I made the drinks that maybe Michael wasn't any happier in the relationship with his brother than Leroy was, that maybe pride might be keeping him from an attempt to make amends. What Michael needed, I decided, was a severe verbal jolt to his overstuffed dignity. And I thought perhaps I knew just the person who was outspoken enough to wield such a blow.

I set the milkshakes on the counter, and after Michael paid me he took them to the other end of the fountain, where he and Linda sat sipping the drinks and exchanging cute glances.

Shortly the store filled with customers seeking refuge from the torrent of rain being unleashed over our tepid city. I was too busy to get back to Leroy, but when he got ready to leave he said he'd be back to pick me up at five, and would I like to take in a new movie that was playing? I didn't want to go to the movie. With Steve's recent news, what I needed was some time alone. But if I put Leroy off I was sure he would be suspicious of my reasons, so I smiled my agreement.

The rain subsided, but the evening still lacked the fun and companionship we usually shared. I couldn't get into the mood of things, though I tried, and I was positive that Leroy took notice.

When we got to my apartment, he said good night at the door and I didn't encourage him to come in. I thanked him for a nice time, we kissed, and I turned to go. Then suddenly I felt his hand touch my arm, and there he was smiling so tenderly at me, his eyes no longer questioning, but accepting, seeming to believe in spite of what he must have felt.

I kissed him again and went inside. But thoughts of the next morning and church with Steve and Noreen wouldn't let sleep come easily. There would be congratulations again to Noreen, and I just didn't like pretending, especially in front of Leroy. It occurred to me then that perhaps I'd been doing a lot of that, and as I offered my nightly prayer to God I begged Him to do something for me, for I knew I couldn't do anything for myself. I fell asleep crying into my pillow.

Chapter 17

I was getting ready to leave for work the next Saturday morning when the phone rang. It was Leroy and he was bubbling over with excitement.

"Do you remember the faith-healing service being held down by the community center?"

"Why, yes, I remember."

"It was supposed to be last month, but there was some delay about getting a permit because of some objections about the location. But they're holding the first service tonight, and, Holly, I'm going!"

"You're going to the faith-healing service?" I asked, dumbfounded.

"I've been praying about it ever since we saw those men erecting the tent. I didn't say anything to you about it because I wanted to be sure. I've never had this kind of faith, not ever in my life, but I have it now, and I'm going to the service. Will you go with me?"

"Yes, of course I'll go. Oh, Leroy, do you really believe that God will heal you?"

"Yes! Yes, I do!"

I was thrilled beyond imagination for Leroy! To think that his faith had progressed so far and so soon! I knew my own had not and maybe never would. Perhaps that was due in part, as I had told Leroy, to the controversy which had so long been a part of faith-healing. So many reputed phonies had hidden behind the Lord's name in that area that my skepticism loomed great—too great, it seemed, for my belief to see me through. But then I'd never been faced with a limitation such as Leroy had.

A thought struck me then. What if the service *was* phony? How could Leroy possibly be healed? A scene from Acts 14 flashed across my mind: In Lystra, where Paul was preaching, was a crippled man who had never been able to walk. He sat there and listened to Paul's words. Paul saw that he had the faith to be healed, so he looked straight at him and said in a loud voice, "Stand up straight on your feet!" And the man jumped up and started walking around.

I found comfort and assurance in that Scripture, for I knew it meant that Leroy's healing would depend on his own faith and not on that of any preacher, whether real or phony.

We arrived early at the tent meeting and went straight down the aisle to the front. Plenty of time remained for prayer before the service began, and we sat with hands clasped and heads bowed.

We weren't very far into the service when I realized that it was much like any other worship experience I'd had. The music was fulfilling, exceptionally so, and following prayer time came the offertory.

The preacher's message was stirring, and when the healing part of the service began I was so filled with excited anticipation I could hardly stay in my seat. I looked over at Leroy. He appeared to be calm and assured. His crutches gripped in his hands before him, he gazed far off at some distant and perhaps imaginary sight. I stared at the aluminum crutches, thinking how wonderful it would be for him if he could really leave the service without them. And he wouldn't need to wear leg braces anymore either.

Sitting quietly beside Leroy, I found myself getting caught up in his belief. It was all he had talked about on the way to the meeting. He was so sure. He truly did believe that God would heal him. I wanted this night so much for Leroy. To be healed of his infirmity was more than I ever dared dream he could have.

Not that he ever complained. In fact, it struck me as a little odd that he was so caught up in being healed all of a sudden. He had never talked of being healed before. I shrugged and decided that although a disabled person had fully dealt with what had come his way, deep inside he must never abandon the hope that his circumstances could change. In Leroy's case, I knew he was sitting there next to me waiting for God to restore the strength in his legs.

We were sitting on aisle seats, and when the preacher called for the afflicted to get up and come out into the aisle, Leroy looked over at me and smiled his beautiful smile, then he squeezed my hand and came slowly to his feet. He made his way into the aisle alongside a number of other people, many of whom were also on crutches and some in wheelchairs. It was a heart-rending sight to see the hope on those shining, trusting faces, and I offered God one last quick prayer for all of them. I was trembling with anticipation when the preacher admonished the group about the sincerity of their belief. Momentarily he called for the lame to be healed in the name of Jesus and for them to get up out of their wheelchairs and put aside their crutches and walk!

My eyes were fastened on Leroy. He propped his crutches against one of the seats and took a few small, slow steps forward. A smile grew on my face. Leroy sometimes went short distances without his crutches, especially in close surroundings such as his kitchen. I was feeling confident because he was doing so well here in this large, open space, but then suddenly when he tried to take another step forward, a much bigger step than before, he lost his balance and would have fallen except for the rapid action of the man seated behind us. The man darted from his chair and grabbed Leroy by the arms. Then he reached over for his crutches. He gave them to Leroy and went quietly back to his seat.

I only caught a glimpse of Leroy's face as he turned and started out the aisle, but that glimpse was enough. I saw more hurting and humiliation there than I ever wanted to see again.

Leroy left the meeting faster than I had ever seen him go anywhere before. My heart was breaking as I hurried out after him. I don't even know if anyone was healed. It seemed that I did see some rejoicing faces, but they didn't register through the tears flowing unbridled down my cheeks.

I lagged behind Leroy, and by the time we reached his car I was beginning to wonder what had gone wrong. His lack of healing had not been because he hadn't believed—of that I was sure. Maybe the preacher was a phony after all, and maybe that had more to do with the situation than I had realized.

Leroy opened the car door for me, but just before I got in I took a quick swipe at my tear-stained face. I didn't want him to see how upset I was. I was afraid it would only add to his hurt. Leroy went around to let himself in, then slid his crutches on the back floor and sank down in the seat beside me. As he lifted his legs with his hands and placed them so heavily beneath the steering wheel, I sensed a difference in his attitude. It was as though he faced a new acceptance of himself, and the resignation he had borne so well was not the same patient submission as before, but a burden heavier to bear than his cumbersome, immobile legs.

Leroy sat quietly behind the wheel of the car for a long time, staring out the front window. Shortly people began to drift out from the tent meeting, and before very much time had passed we were alone in a deserted parking lot. It was then that Leroy finally spoke.

"I made a fool of myself tonight."

"No—"

He was nodding as he turned to face me. "The reason God didn't heal me was not because I didn't believe. I believed. Oh, yes, I believed—but for the wrong reason."

"For what...reason?"

Leroy gazed levelly at me for another long time. It seemed for a while that he wanted to speak, but the words just wouldn't come. Then finally, "I wanted to be healed...so I could... compete for you."

"Compete for me?"

"So I could compete with Steve."

He said it so smoothly, so casually, that I shouldn't have been taken aback at all. But I was. My mouth fell open and I was certain my face went pale. Leroy was still gazing steadily at me and I knew he could read my thoughts.

For a while I couldn't speak either. I didn't know what to say. A denial of my feelings would have been useless and ridiculous, not to mention an assault on Leroy's intelligence. But I had to spare his feelings if I could, and I wanted to clear up a part of what he said.

"Leroy, you know I'm not the least bit turned off because you're crippled, so why do you think you need good legs to...well, for any reason?"

"To compete with Steve."

"No."

"You mean you aren't going to admit that we're in competition?"

"You aren't in competition."

"No, I suppose not."

There was so much pain in his voice that it brought stinging tears to my eyes again. I blinked them quickly away. "You don't understand."

"I understand...too well."

"You aren't in any competition with Steve. How could you be? You know he and Noreen are getting married next month." Even as I spoke the words, they tore bitterly at my heart.

"I'm not trying to compete with his place in your *life*—only his place in your *heart*."

"No. You two aren't even in the same ball park."

Leroy's face collapsed, and I was suddenly seeing again all the hurt and humiliation that he had carried from the faith-healing service. "Please, Holly, I am a human being. I may be a freak, like Michael says, but I still have feelings."

"Oh, stop it! I won't even listen to that!" I turned away but I could feel Leroy's eyes upon me, burning, searing. "You know what I meant. Steve is my friend. That's one thing. You are...you...are something else.''

"Are you saying you don't love Steve? Because if you are, you needn't bother. I can feel it when you're together. I know he's only your friend, but you're in love with him—I know that, too.''

I sat facing the window. I was unable to speak. It seemed as if the world were caving in all around me as Leroy's words pounded uncontrollably in my ears.

"Holly, turn around and look at me.''

How could I look at him now? Everything about me would bear witness to what he had said. Suddenly I felt Leroy reach for me. When I felt his gentle touch on my shoulder and heard him softly call my name, I turned. His face was a picture of love and tenderness, but in his eyes I could still see the hurt and anguish.

"Steve and I are very good friends, yes, but that's all.''

"Can you tell me you don't love him?''

I knew I couldn't, but I didn't say anything. Then without warning I felt a surge of anger rush within me. What Leroy was doing really wasn't fair after all. He had no right. I couldn't help how I felt. I certainly hadn't been guilty of any real deceit. I had only tried to spare Leroy any pain. Steve didn't love me, not in the same way I loved him, so what was I supposed to do, sit home and not share myself with anyone?

"You've never so much as hinted at this before,'' I accused.

"It's been coming...for a long time,'' Leroy replied, his voice heavy with despair. "I've felt it ever since the night at the hospital when you introduced me to Steve. I guess I just hoped I was wrong, but every time Steve was around you were different. And the day at the candy shop when he came to tell you he was getting married...well, how could I not know? But even then I tried, I really tried—and I still hoped."

Yes, I guess I knew it had been coming, too. I had only hoped it wouldn't because I knew how it would spoil everything. "Maybe it would have been better if you'd never told me."

"But how could I ever be sure? I'd always wonder if you were looking at me and thinking of him."

"The way I see it that's your problem." I choked back bitter tears. "I'm not going to say I'm sorry. I haven't done anything to be sorry for, and I think I'm more than a little hurt that you don't have any faith in me. How could you think I'd do such a thing as purposely deceive you?"

"It's the last thing I want to think," he said, his tone genuine with remorse.

"What did you want me to do, confess this undying love after our first date? How would that have made you feel?"

"I don't know. Maybe you could have said something to let me know I was wasting my time."

"Who ever said you were wasting your time?"

Leroy greeted my comment with a long, silent stare. I tried then to explain exactly the way it was between Steve and me—the wonderful trust and Christian friendship we shared—but I could tell by the torn expression on his face that it couldn't appease his hurt. And the more I thought about it, the more I could see it his way—but there just wasn't anything I could do to change the facts. I loved Steve and I always would.

"So where do we go from here?" I asked forlornly.

Leroy shrugged and looked away. I touched his arm. "I wish you hadn't done this to us. What we had was so beautiful."

He turned, his clear eyes flashing angrily. "What I did to us? What about you?"

"But what have I done? I loved a man before I ever met you. What kind of crime is that?"

"You're still in love with him!"

"But I...I love you, too!" The words just tumbled out, brokenly, stupidly. And I was amazed at the change in my boldness, though I still knew my words were true. And it wasn't just a feeling that they were true, although that was certainly plain enough to me all of a sudden, for love and tenderness toward Leroy encompassed me, but it was more than that. It was something concrete, but I couldn't get it in perspective at that moment.

"I don't want to be loved—too. I just want to be loved."

"But I do love you! I do!"

He pulled me close and his soft words poured tenderly, lovingly over my aching heart. "Do you really, Holly, do you?"

"Yes, I do," I said, gazing into his eyes, so beautiful, so entreating.

He touched my face and began stroking my cheek. He ran his fingers gently along my arm. "I love to touch you. I've never loved anything so much." He smothered me in his arms and gave me such an ardent kiss I thought my lips would burst beneath his passion. "If only you knew how much I love and want you," he whispered, and kissed me again and again.

I was aflame in his arms, and it was beyond my reasoning how he could doubt my love. Later I told him so.

He drew abruptly away and sat staring out the window. "But it can't be this way."

"It is this way."

"No." He turned. "You can't love both of us."

"But I do."

"You have to make a choice."

"I don't have any choice to make. Steve doesn't want me. He's happy and I'm happy for him."

"What if he did want you?" he said, and his tone was eager and agitated now.

His words fell heavily on my ears. I had never thought of it that way, probably because I knew after Steve met Noreen he would never feel the kind of love for me that I felt for him.

"If you could be with Steve, would you have ever started dating me?"

"That's not fair."

"Why isn't it? Just because he doesn't feel as strongly as you do doesn't stop the way you feel, does it?"

I couldn't answer Leroy. But I didn't have to.

"You have to make the choice in your heart."

"I've done that. I've just realized how much I love you."

"But I still share your heart with someone else."

"How do I stop what's in my heart?"

Leroy looked at me with all hopelessness in his blue eyes, and I knew we were right back where we'd started.

When we got back to my apartment, Leroy saw me to the door and kissed me tenderly good night. I asked him when I'd see him again, but he said he didn't know.

I hadn't been inside my apartment more than a few minutes when it occurred to me that Leroy and I hadn't finished discussing one important aspect of what he'd told me. I still didn't understand why he felt he had to be a more complete man physically in order to, as he put it, "compete with Steve." I knew his attitude about his limitation. He had accepted it beautifully and had much confidence in himself. If it had once made him feel inadequate in the area of his personal life, our relationship had changed that. He had told me so himself. So what was the problem?

As I prepared for bed that night, Leroy's obvious feelings of inadequacy were a grave concern upon my heart. Maybe I was still more a part of it than I realized. Perhaps he was making more of my relationship with Steve because of his disability, but I couldn't understand the urgency that had led him to the faith-healing service. Before crawling between the covers, I offered myself to God in prayer, asking Him to show me a way to resolve the dilemma in Leroy's troubled heart and mine.

Chapter 18

When I had asked God to help Leroy and me resolve our problems, I hadn't expected His solution to come in exactly the way that it did. The week following the faith-healing service I didn't see or hear from Leroy. He didn't call me or come by my apartment, and he didn't come to the candy shop for hot fudge sundaes or to pick me up at closing time.

I was tempted to give him a call. Many times, alone in my apartment, I went to the telephone, but always I walked away without disturbing it. While working at the candy shop, it would have been so easy to walk down to the bank. I started to on several occasions, but decided at the last minute that both Leroy and I needed the time apart to come to some decisions. The only problem was that I wasn't coming to any. Steve and his upcoming wedding wasn't on my mind as much, but that was because I was too busy wondering about Leroy. Once I almost asked Linda Benton about her boss, and I even thought of asking Michael about him, but later I was glad that I hadn't.

I didn't tell anyone about the faith-healing service, and I didn't mention that Leroy and I hadn't seen each other since that night. Both Cara and Bertha questioned me about Leroy's absence from the shop, but I avoided an explanation by saying that he was probably having an unusually busy week. This didn't fool Bertha, of course, but for once she didn't probe me with her piercing doubts and questions.

It was the next Thursday that I got home from work and found Leroy's letter in the mailbox.

> My Dearest Holly,
>
> Knowing your respect for the written word, I thought you would understand why I chose to tell you what's on my heart by writing this letter. It's not that I'm too much of a coward to face you; I think you know that's not true. It's just that I could never say good-bye face to face. I can't look at you and do much of anything except look at you and want to touch you.
>
> I've done a lot of thinking and praying about us, and since it was my hope that we would one day be married, you will understand with how much sorrow I'm writing these words.
>
> I've left the bank. I've sublet my apartment and taken a position with a small bank in Cedarville.

It was difficult to leave my home and place of employment, but I discussed my decision with Mom and Dad and received their blessing. It was through Dad's long friendship with the Cedarville bank president that I was able to apply for this job. We have kept it all a secret until you will have time to receive this letter.

It was very hard to leave "The Maria Elena," but it isn't such a long drive from here to the lake for weekend sailing until winter comes soon.

Most of all, it was all I could do to leave you, my lovely Holly, especially without saying goodbye. You made my life more beautiful than I ever dreamed it could be, and it was your precious faith that caused me to truly seek my Lord. I can never thank you adequately for that.

My work here is challenging and I'm sure I will be happy. Everyone is so kind and I know I will make new friends. Please pray for me and I will always pray for you. And please don't be angry with me for going away like this. Try to understand that I could not go on seeing you the way things were, and if I'd stayed there I would not have been able to stay away from you.

I continue to pray for your work with Johanna. I know it is just a matter of time until the book is published.

I miss you more than you will ever know.

All my love and devotion,
Leroy

I read Leroy's letter through again and then thrust myself

upon the bed and lay there crying till it seemed that no more tears would come. I had caused Leroy untold personal heartache. I had caused him to give up his job, his home, his boat, and even, I knew, his work with HAL, although he hadn't mentioned that.

It was the knowledge of all I'd done to him that kept me from climbing into my car and racing over to Cedarville. I had done enough to mess up his life, and since I couldn't offer him my whole heart and single-minded love, I had no right to go barging in on his new life and make that miserable too.

I filled the lonely days apart from Leroy with my job at the candy shop and the mornings' work with Johanna. The book continued to progress well despite the anguish in my heart and mind. To fill the solemn nights, I began taking our notes and those Johanna had kept over the years and shaping them into a story form.

Yet some evenings my hands and mind just would not work. On those nights I put on the record album Leroy had given me and sat listening and counting my losses. I knew better. I knew I should have been counting my blessings, but as the plaintive croon poured softly from the stereo I felt sorry for myself. I had lost both my mother and my father. I had lost Steve (in a manner of speaking), and now Leroy.

It was an unhappy September, but throughout the month it seemed that even the lonely nights went better than the days. There was never a time when the door of the candy shop jingled open that I didn't look up, expecting, hoping, to see Leroy. I thought again of quitting my job at the shop, but that enchanting place was so filled with blissful memories of Leroy that I couldn't bear to leave. Memories were all I had now, and I clung to them with an almost-desperate fervor.

Often I wondered if Leroy missed me as I missed him, how

could he possibly stay away? But I knew all too well that most of his life had been spent abiding his circumstances beyond his control and that he wasn't about to weaken in the face of a situation over which he did have some power and had exerted it.

Leroy's sudden and clandestine departure from the bank sent a flurry of suspicious rumors about the neighborhood. To my knowledge his father offered no explanation other than word that Leroy had taken a new and challenging position with a smaller bank in a town not too far away. Even Michael didn't seem to know why Leroy had rushed off so secretly, but it didn't appear to bother him unduly. He questioned me once or twice, but I had taken a very taciturn attitude. I had practically been forced into it. Bertha queried me so much at first that it became all but impossible to speak of Leroy and keep profuse tears from burning my eyes at the same time.

No one in our little downtown community, however, was in any way fooled into thinking that Leroy's unexpected departure had nothing to do with me. Nor did I expect them to. When our regular customers came in the shop, their faces completely burst with curiosity at first, and I sought to find a way to appease their natural inclinations to wonder, but I couldn't come up with any truthful explanation that would protect Leroy's dignity and guard my feelings for Steve. So I said nothing and gradually talk died down. I knew no one meant to be unkind, and finally I decided it was really no one's business and let it go at that.

October dawned bright and colorful to find me in an emotional shambles. The first week dragged by painfully, and then it was a scant two weeks till Steve and Noreen's wedding. It was on a Saturday that I struggled so terribly about whether I would be able to attend or not. Their lovely invitation had arrived in the mail only that morning, and I sat reading the delicate inscription and weeping uncontrollably.

Leroy had been gone for over a month. At the same time that I was battling with my feelings for Steve, I was longing deeply for Leroy. How I missed his sweet companionship and tender expressions of love! There wasn't any doubt that I had come to love him very much, although I still couldn't place what it was that made me so positive. It was more than just the way I felt—it was some evidence in actual existence. I loved Leroy and I loved Steve. How could I truly love them both? Perhaps Leroy had found a solution to our dilemma (at least outwardly), but it certainly seemed that I had not. I grew more miserable with each passing day.

It was at this point that it occurred to me how ridiculous the whole situation was. Steve was marrying someone else and there was absolutely nothing I could do about it, nor did I really want to. And there was Leroy, off someplace that he didn't want to be; and here I was, alone and lonely, when I could have been with the man I loved—one of them, at least. Why couldn't it be the way it had been before? But no, Leroy was right. Steve could be with Noreen, but Leroy couldn't be with me, not until he held the same place in my heart that he held by my side. Suddenly a horrifying thought struck me. Very soon I would not only be a young woman in love with two men, but a young woman in love with a man who was married!

I knew only God could save me from such a fate. On my knees I pleaded with Him not to let such a sinful situation happen. I guess I was asking for a miracle, for I had no thought of my own how I could ever stop loving Steve.

When Steve and Noreen's wedding day arrived, I decided there was no way I could graciously decline to attend short of becoming ill. With the state of my emotions, that didn't seem to be a great impossibility, but the fact never materialized and

I reached church completely decked out and in plenty of time to get a good seat.

Alone in a long wooden pew and tenderly wrapped in soft organ music, several feelings rushed over me all at the same time. First, I didn't know how I could possibly sit there and watch Steve marry someone else. It would make me both happy and sad to see his joy. I had been grappling with this emotion since the day Steve came to the candy shop and told me that he and Noreen had decided to get married. Though I was only minutes away from witnessing that sacred scene, I seemed to be an eternity away from knowing how to handle it. Then a feeling came over me I couldn't understand. I had begun to feel so alone sitting in my own church. I had gotten used to Leroy being with me and I missed him terribly, but it had not bothered me as much as it did at that moment.

Suddenly the wedding march began. Following the entrance of the attendants, everyone stood up for the bride's procession. It was when Noreen stepped into the aisle that I experienced the strangest feeling of all. She came forward, a beautiful picture in her gown of flowing white, and then Steve came across the front to join her, so handsome in his dark tuxedo. Tears welled up in my eyes and spilled in great drops onto my cheeks. But they were not tears of hurt or sorrow. Only tears of relief and ecstacy! Everything I thought I'd feel at the sight of these two on their special day seemed to be washed away in the flood of my tears. Every part of me purely rejoiced for them and I could not have been happier if it had been Leroy and me.

Leroy and me! But that was it! That was the only thing missing. Leroy was not at my side. I experienced a fresh outpouring of tears, and I knew that God had answered my prayers. The desire to be with Leroy filled me utterly then. There was no room left even for Steve. At that moment I knew I was over my love for Steve, that his place in my heart had been taken by my love for Leroy. From the bottom of my soul, I knew that somehow in the near future there must be another special day in our church, one with another bride and groom, but this time the groom would be on crutches.

After the reception in the dining hall in the basement of the church, I went home to my apartment with my heart much at ease. I prepared for bed and settled down to write a "letter" to God. I had not done that for a while, since I had begun work on Johanna's book. And I had so much to thank Him for that night.

On impulse, I picked up the folder of letters that I had been keeping all summer and began to read. To my amazement, I discovered that Steve's name hardly appeared anywhere in all those many pages. There were prayers for him, for his well-being, for God's will in his life, but there was nothing different written about him from what was written for any other Christian friend. What did fill those pages were prayers and thoughts of Leroy. I had written about everything we had done and about all his kind gestures and sweet ways. I had prayed for the Holy Spirit to have His way with him; I had prayed for his health, his work, his family, his relationship with Michael, his friends, HAL—everything that was connected in any way with Leroy. At the close of each night's entries I had thanked God for sending him into my life.

So here was my proof, the evidence in actual existence. It all became clear to me then. I had loved Leroy for a long time and didn't even know it! I never thought I could love anyone after Steve, but Leroy had shown me how wrong I was. Suddenly I smiled in remembrance. Only Holly had been fooled!

God had known, too, of course, and had used Steve and

Noreen's wedding to make me realize it. Oh, how good He was, and how weak was my faith in Him!

I tucked the neatly penned pages back into the folder and returned it to the drawer. What I had to say that night was not meant for the written word, nor was it meant for God alone to hear. But first there was something else I had to take care of.

Chapter 19

I found Michael in his office. I don't know why that surprised me except that I had always pictured him doing something silly all the time, like running around the steno pool, laughing his pretentious laugh and flirting outrageously with the typists. I smiled to myself. I supposed Linda Benton kept him from doing much of that. And his father.

I knocked softly at the door, and when Michael called for me to come in, I could tell that he was shocked to see me. He got up immediately from a high-backed leather chair and came around a broad, polished desk that was laden with assorted papers.

"Well, Holly baby, to what do I owe the good fortune of this visit? Have you finally decided you want a real man instead of a cri—"

"No!" I cried, cutting him off as rapidly as I could. I wasn't about to stand there and let him put Leroy down another time. I hadn't been able to think of one good thing about Leroy being gone—I hadn't even tried—but all of a sudden one grand reason popped into my head. And if I had known before about how I was going to boldly confront Michael, I knew at that moment that whatever I said I had to somehow say *something,* anything, that would stop his lifetime of insults. But I knew that before I could do this I had to change his attitude. Right there, standing in front of Michael in his plush office of thick carpet and expensive wood, I had a short, silent conversation with God.

"Lord, you and I both know that I can't do a thing about Michael's attitude—only You are in the changing business. But, please, Lord, if You can use me to help bring this about, then use me now."

"Well, all right," Michael said, "what did you come up here for?"

"I came...I came to talk to you," I faltered.

Michael plopped onto the corner of his dark, polished desk. "Sure thing, baby." He pointed toward a black leather chair nearby. "Have a seat."

I walked the few steps to the chair and sank down, trying to further collect my thoughts. This wasn't going to be an easy task, I mused, not so sure of myself as I once was. I had gone over in my mind a thousand times exactly what I wanted to say to Leroy's brother, but now that I was face to face with him all my composed thoughts seemed to have vanished. Perhaps I was having second thoughts about confronting him, and that could be just as well.

How would he take what I hoped to get across to him? How would he react to a third party intruding upon the little game he had been playing? Or was it a game? When I imparted my news, would he turn on me in a rage? Was he really sick of mind, a little off-balance mentally? Could I actually help bring about a healing in the broken relationship between Leroy and Michael? Or was I treading on dangerous territory, about to bring Michael's uncertain wrath down upon my head? There seemed only one way to find out. In a minute I lifted my eyes to Michael's steady, carefree gaze.

"You know Leroy and I haven't been seeing each other these last few weeks. He went away...he took that other job...well...he left because of me."

"What's that got to do with me?" Michael asked, laughing at me with his enormous brown eyes.

I smiled inwardly. Michael's first thoughts were always of himself. "I'm going to see Leroy this weekend. I'm going to see him and tell him I want to marry him...that is, if he will still have me."

"So?"

"Well, that's sort of what I want to talk to you about. If Leroy and I should get married, I'm sure your parents would want a big wedding and well...you and...Leroy..."

"What about me and Leroy?"

I looked down at my lap. I had been folding and unfolding my hands without realizing it. I relaxed and directed my attention to Michael's questioning gaze. "Do you think you could keep from saying anything insulting to Leroy?"

"Ol' Leroy? Are you kidding? He doesn't—"

"I know all about the things you did to Leroy," I blurted out. "He told me about when you were kids and how you used to go off with his crutches and leave him down in the woods, and how you hit him in the stomach that time so hard till he got sick and—"

I stopped, suddenly realizing that Michael's face had taken on a stricken look. He looked as though *he* had been stricken with a dreadful disease. His mouth fell open and his eyebrows shot up and the deepest wave of pain twisted his handsome features. But I think the worst effect of my words took place in his eyes. So large and round and dark, they clouded over like an evening sky before a summer storm. He looked as though his entire life were passing before him, and for a minute I thought he was actually going to break down and cry.

He got up then and walked around the desk and stood gazing out a huge window. I didn't know what to do next, whether to go on or not. I chose not to, and sat waiting for him to penetrate the silence. I didn't think he was ever going to.

"Leroy used to fall down a lot," he said, his back to me, "when he was first learning how to walk again. I used to laugh at him when he fell. Then I'd run and hide in my room and I'd cry till I was sobbing. I wasn't very old, but I remember doing that."

Michael paused in what he was saying, and I could tell he was reliving painful memories. Immediately I thought I'd made a mistake in confronting him, that perhaps I should leave. I considered what he might say as too personal, too heart-rending for the spoken word. But before I could speak or get up he went on.

"Leroy was always a good kid. He never did talk back or anything and he always helped out a lot. I never got into any serious trouble, but I was pretty much a rascal. I was always into some mischief or the other.

"It was rotten what happened to Leroy. He didn't deserve

it. No kid did. But Leroy took it—he took everything. He wasn't a coward. It takes a whole lot more guts to accept what life deals you, the part you can't change, and go on, than it does to lash out. I was the coward. I lashed out. I wanted to fix things for Leroy. I wanted to make him like he used to be, like my big brother that I adored, but I didn't know how, and I didn't realize that I couldn't anyway. And I used to think if such a thing could happen to a good kid like Leroy, what could happen to me?

"When we were kids, I took my fear out on Leroy, and instead of acting like I felt way down inside, I did the opposite: I struck out at the object of what I really wanted to do something for. And I guess I resented Leroy, too. I resented the extra attention he got for a while, and I never liked what he had become. I didn't like to think that such a thing as being crippled could happen to anybody. But I saw him every day wearing those steel braces and swinging himself around on crutches. He seemed like some kind of hideous monster, and I thought I hated him."

Michael shrugged. "But what did I know? I was just a stupid kid."

"You're not a kid anymore."

Michael turned around and looked at me. "When we got a little older and I understood better what Leroy had suffered and still suffers, I mean because he's a crip—because he can't use his legs—I tried to cover up what I felt and what I'd done. I couldn't let anybody know. So I just kept picking at Leroy. It was so easy because he never fought back."

"He couldn't."

"He could do more than you think. He was solid as a rock and strong as an ox from all the therapy, but he didn't even try to fight me with words. Once he did try to talk to me, but I was so ashamed by then that I couldn't deal with it. I was the one who'd become a monster."

I studied Michael's attractive features. He was sincere in what he was saying, I could tell. I sensed that he was really glad to share his feelings with me, with someone at last. He spoke like a man profoundly relieved to finally be able to share an over-whelming burden. I believed he really wanted to get rid of his guilt, and I sat quietly thanking God for using me. I had found out that Michael was a human being after all and that his true feelings had just been deeply buried for a long time. He wasn't sick in the head, as I had suspected. Neither did he seem to have such bad personality flaws now that his guilt was out in the open.

Michael came around the desk and stood before me. "I remember right after Leroy got polio, when he was trying to learn how to use the muscles in his legs again, he'd break out in a sweat from trying so hard and because it hurt so much. But no matter how much it hurt, he never cried, he never made a sound. I think that's partly why I didn't realize for a long time what a living hell he went through. Mom and Dad tried to explain to me how difficult the therapy was, but I didn't understand.

"And then when Leroy and Mom and Dad and the doctors finally realized that all his struggling had been for nothing, Leroy still didn't complain about losing the use of his legs. He just accepted the fact that to walk again he would have to go through more therapy and learn how to walk using braces and crutches. He just went on to do what he had to do and he never seemed to blame anything or anyone."

Michael stopped talking and his face took on a different expression. He suddenly reminded me of Leroy.

"Inside I really admire Leroy and I'm sorry for every-thing I've done to him. I don't know why I've let it go on so long—a habit, I guess, putting him down.''

"I guess I'm really not the one you should be telling."

"You think he'll listen...now?"

I smiled gently. "I know he will."

A great relief rushed through my heart as I got up to leave Michael's office. I felt I had done the right thing in helping him to share his true self after so many years of pretending to be a person that he was not.

He walked with me to the door, and though some of the arrogance was still there in his grace and manner, I believed that in time even those qualities would become more subdued. I caught a trace of the hidden charm I had noticed in him once before, and as I offered him my handshake, friends at last, he held my hand in his for a long moment.

"If you want to see Leroy this weekend, you better go out to Mom and Dad's. He called them last night and said he was coming to see them and take his boat out."

"Will you be going out there?"

"Leroy said he was driving over tonight. I think I'll go out right after work."

"Then I'll wait till tomorrow. You two need this night."

Chapter 20

I drove out to the Britton home late Saturday afternoon after work. Michael had told Leroy that I was coming and that I had something important to tell him. When I arrived, Leroy met me at the door. With gentle and complete love, our eyes met and time seemed to stand still. Then Leroy took me in his arms for a kiss I would never forget. His lingering touch told me how deeply he had missed me, and in his lasting embrace I confirmed every answer my heart had been searching for.

We spent a few minutes in polite conversation with Mr. and Mrs. Britton and Michael, and I couldn't help but notice the pride in Michael's dark eyes. I could tell he was truly happy that Leroy and I were together again. We excused ourselves to go for a walk by the lake, with a promise to return later for dinner. As we were departing, Michael left to pick up Linda Benton. He, too, promised they would come back for the evening meal. I sensed that this was a monumental event in the lives of the elder Brittons, having both their sons compatibly at the dinner table with the young ladies of their choosing.

The autumn evening was one of breathtaking loveliness as Leroy and I walked beside the cool waters of Lake Wyeth. The trees, in myriad colors of red and gold and orange, were etched in the distance against a pale, cloudless sky. A gentle breeze stirred, and birds fluttered now and then overhead.

I glanced up at Leroy as we walked along, not knowing where to begin. Finally I burst out with how wrong I had been all the time, and told him what took place inside me at Steve and Noreen's wedding.

"Steve will always have a special place in my heart. It wouldn't be fair of me not to tell you that, but I don't love him, not the way I love you, not now. You've changed all that."

"I told myself I was coming out here to see Mom and Dad and take 'The Maria Elena' out, but if Michael hadn't told me you were coming today I'd have come to see you and tell you how wrong I was and how foolish I'd been for going away."

"I don't think it was so foolish. It gave us a chance to get a new perspective on things."

"After I left I did a lot more thinking about us, and I realized something I had refused to see before. Steve was there first—in your heart I mean, and in your life too—and you were right, I didn't have any right to question it. How could you know that I didn't have someone who meant a great deal to me before I knew you? I think just about everyone has a special someone that they will always hold dear. I just happened to come along at a time in your life to know about your someone."

"You were partly right, too. I did need to straighten out my feelings."

"I was ready to accept your feelings whatever they were."

"Leroy, you never did tell me why you felt you had to be healed to compete with Steve."

We went along in silence. Leroy's answer didn't come for a while. "It was that first night at church with you. We were getting ready to leave when Steve and Noreen came up, and Steve reached over and picked up your books and purse and offered to carry them for you. And there I stood...I couldn't... well, you know. I thought I should've been doing that for you."

I stopped in our stroll and Leroy drew up beside me. I reached up and touched his cheek lightly with the tips of my fingers, the way you touch something very precious. I smiled, letting the love and tenderness I felt for him show completely. "My darling Leroy, don't you know little things like that don't matter at all?"

"I know, but I want you to have little things like that. You deserve to have them. You deserve more than I can give."

"I don't want any more."

"That night at church made me wonder if I really have a right to ask you, or any woman, to share my life. It's a lot to ask someone to share your life when it includes a disability like mine."

"Don't you think that's a decision the woman has to make?"

"You deserve a whole man."

"You're a whole man."

"But I'm a crip—"

I touched my fingers to his lips, stopping the flow of his words. "You know it doesn't matter." I went up on tiptoe and kissed him with all the desire and caring in my heart.

When we had resumed our walk, Leroy spoke again. "To get your brother and your girl back all in the same weekend, that's a lot for a man." He glanced over at me, smiling grandly. "Michael told me what you said to him."

"I'm glad everything's all right between you two now." I gave him back a smile and we went along quietly, thinking our own thoughts.

Finally Leroy broke the stillness. "Before I moved into my apartment, I used to love to get up early and come out on the patio and watch the deer coming out of the woods to get a drink from the lake. I like the unspoiled beauty of it. Someday I'd like to build a house by this lake. I think out away from the city is the best place to raise kids, don't you?"

I nodded.

"How do you feel about kids, Holly?"

"I don't go along with the current trend—I don't want any till I'm married."

A beautiful smile graced Leroy's gentle lips. It was sunshine in autumn. "I'm not sure I'd make a good father—there'd be some things I couldn't do with my kids."

"You'd be a wonderful father! You'd give them what they need most—plenty of love."

"Look!" Leroy cried suddenly and stopped walking.

I drew up next to him, gazing toward the never-ending sky. The late evening sun was sprawled in the misty white heavens like orange glaze on a billowy cake. Below, the blazing colors of the trees had turned almost black and stood out vividly against the backdrop of a fiery sky.

"The sun sure is beautiful out over the water and trees like that, isn't it?"

"It's so beautiful it almost defies description."

"I bet you could come up with a way to describe it. Writers always can."

I smiled, responding with a deep sense of satisfaction that we both shared.

Leroy turned and gazed longingly into my eyes. "Just about everything I hold dear is right here. I can reach out and touch it, almost all of it."

We stared quietly and tenderly at each other for a long time.

"Would you like to live in that house with me?" Leroy said at last.

"Is that a proposal?"

"Yes."

"I'd love to live in that house with you."

"I could never take you dancing."

"I can always go with Michael."

Leroy smiled his sunny smile again. "Holly, look at me. This is what I am and what I'll always be."

"Not *always.*"

"You know what I mean."

"And you know how I feel about that."

"I just want you to be sure, because there's a current trend I don't go along with. I believe marriage is forever."

Like my father, I thought. "I'm sure. I'm absolutely sure."

He gazed at me out of eyes that wanted so much to believe. "Tell me again."

I grinned mischievously and reached for him, pulling his face down near mine. We kissed and then suddenly I threw my head back and laughed. The sun had gone down, but I could see it still in Leroy's jubilant face.

Always!